THE KID ON SLAPTON BEACH

Felicity Fair Thompson

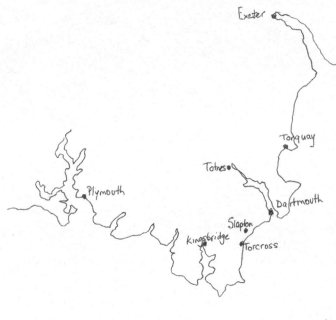

THE KID ON SLAPTON BEACH

Felicity Fair Thompson

WIGHT DIAMOND PRESS

THE KID ON SLAPTON BEACH

This story is dedicated to the
bravery and sacrifice of the ordinary people
and the Allied troops involved in this difficult
episode of the Second World War.

Acknowledgements

My thanks to both Beverley Birch, former Senior Editor Hodder Children's Books, and to Anna Home, Chair of the Children's Film and Television Foundation for their encouragement and belief in this story.

I am most grateful to ALCS and the Writers' Guild for their help and advice on permissions and to Jane Tatam for her support and guidance with publication.

My thanks to Orchard Publications, and author Robin Rose-Price for advice on available images, and to the Dartmouth Museum for allowing use of the photographs on the cover from their extensive collection.

Chapter One

'We have to clear out, Mum. Families, shops, farmers, everyone!'

The shock on his mother's face frightened Harry. She abandoned the sink of soapy washing.

'What?'

Amy burst in behind him. 'He's been on that beach again, Celia!' she said, sinking into a kitchen chair. 'I've never seen a boy more covered in sand!'

'I ran back that way!' Harry protested, brushing himself down, wondering why sand mattered when his mother was trembling?

'Leave our homes, Amy?' His mother's wet hands smeared urgently down her apron.

Harry nodded. 'By the twentieth of December.'

'What! Before Christmas?' Celia stared at Amy.

Amy mopped her face with her handkerchief. 'I know. Less than two weeks! They want all the coast, and inland too...'

'But where do we go?' said Celia.

'What about Daddy?' Harry asked, but his mother's frightened eyes were still on her friend.

'Wherever we can,' said Amy. 'We can come back in six months, nine at the most. The farmers are up in arms at being pushed off their land.'

'We lose our field work?' Celia cried. 'Oh, Amy, with my John missing I really need that money.'

'And where's our food going to come from without land?' demanded Amy. 'Old Abraham Thorn, he shakes his walking stick at the Warden and the others. Not me, says he! Not for the enemy, and not for GIs! In seventy-eight years I've never left this village. The only way I'll go now is in a wooden box!'

'The poor old man!'

Peppy let out a shriek wanting to be lifted out of her cot. Harry offered his little sister his finger instead. Her pursed lips closed round it and sand stuck to her top lip. 'But if old Mr Thorn won't go...' Peppy's sharp little teeth bit into his finger. He snatched it away. 'Ow!'

'Ssh, Harry, be quiet!' snapped his mother.

'The land is requisitioned.' Amy held up the leaflet. 'The 1939 Regulations. Some Government Act or other passed when we first went to war. There's no arguing with it now. They are coming and that's that. Of course, the main man says, like butter wouldn't melt in his mouth, you'd all like to stay in your homes until the last possible day, but those who go first will get the best accommodation and the best transport.' She pushed herself to her feet and made for the door.

Celia followed her. 'You're my best friend, Amy. Where will you go?'

'I have an aunt in Exeter somewhere. And there's my Jack's old dad to worry about too.' She patted Celia's arm. 'We'll keep in touch, don't you worry. I'm off now to see what's happening to the church organ.'

'What if there's no one we know? Nowhere to go?'

But Amy had no answer.

Back at the kitchen sink his mother plunged her hands back into the hot water. She was crying.

'What's going to happen?' Harry asked nervously.

'Oh, Harry, I don't know, do I?' She wiped a wet hand across her forehead. 'We're at war.'

Peppy began to cry. Harry felt his little sister's despair. 'She's hungry,' he said.

He picked up the leaflet. The words on it were in thick, black print.

NOTICE: December 1943

Every person must leave the area by 20th of this month. The supply of electricity will cease the following day. The present measures for supplying food will finish. The police stations are closing this week. Information centres will remain open until the following day... and it listed telephone numbers and other stuff...

The public are reminded requisition has already taken effect, and the Admiralty may at any time and without notice enforce their right to immediate possession.

'Mum, what will happen when Daddy comes back? Will he know where to find us?'

But his mother was nodding to herself. 'Lewis,' she muttered. 'I'll ask Lewis. He'll know what to do!'

Harry flung the leaflet down. 'You can't ask him!' He bolted to his room. Behind him his little sister exploded into full scream.

Chapter Two

Harry sat fingering the treasures on his bedside table. Smooth pebbles. Pieces of dark slate. Shiny iridescent shells, the skeleton of a spider crab, smooth white bones of birds. And the framed photograph of Daddy. That was always comfortingly near at night. Now the face behind the glass seemed unreachable, disappearing, like a trick of the light.

'Harry?'

He leapt off the bed and flung open his window. The fresh salt sea air was enticing.

'Come and mind Peppy. I'm going out. Harry?'

Two seconds and he was out and away, running down the lane towards the beach. Behind him his mother leaned out his window. 'Harry Beere! Come back here! I told you, I'm going out!'

By the derelict seafront hotel metal poles and huge rolled tangles of wire bit deep into the sand to stop invaders from the sea. A sign on a rusting iron barrier read: Danger! Landmines! Strictly no entry! A fisherman's dog had been blown up along there.

Harry squinted along the coast road. Two US army lorries were driving in, coming to the two tiny villages, Torcross here by the beach, and Slapton, behind the lagoon, the Ley. Only green farmland rose up from there. What did the Americans want with any of it?

He looked out across the choppy grey sea. Dark clouds were bubbling up. Somewhere over there was the war. Somewhere in Italy his daddy was missing. He grabbed a stone and hurled it as far out into the sea as he could. The glistening waves swallowed it and headed in relentlessly towards him.

It was cheerful walking along the sand dunes. The winter sun was low now and the wind had dropped. Gulls wheeled lazily overhead. Down on the shore the waves dragged out, and rattled in again across the shifting pebbles.

Harry squinted inland, took his bearings from the old tower, lining it up with the ruined hotel. Four long steps. A jump down onto rock. Two more long steps to that clump of bushes. Pushing them aside, he slid down through the hole underneath. The bushes sprang back, sprinkling sand down on top of him like salt.

Nobody else knew this cave was here. Not

even Mum. He and Daddy only found it by chance. Rock overhead, sandy floor; light filtering in where smaller rocks jutted together, forming a sort of window. This was their secret place, their Sunday headquarters, where they scanned the sea for ships, and watched gulls strutting close enough to for them to count every feather. They talked about climbing rocks, and doing handstands, fixing the old beach boats, fishing, and all the different fish to catch, and then always, racing each other back along the shore so they wouldn't be late for tea. Harry ran a finger over two sets of initials in the smooth stone, the rough edges of an HB next to a JHB. He pictured Dad's fair hair falling over his forehead, and his strong hands pushing up the sloppy sleeves of his old grey sweater as he gouged the letters out with a penknife. He could hear his laugh, and remember his eyes, blue as the bay in summer, and his words that day: 'We're carving ourselves into this beach now, son. Don't see us ever leaving here, do you?'

But the night the bomb dropped, Daddy said nobody could feel safe, not even in a tiny coastal village like this. Long into that night Harry heard him talking about doing his bit, and Mum crying. The British army uniform he came home in next day, made of rough khaki cloth, gave him a stiff, tall, official look. But in the crowds at the station, after he patted Mum's tummy and kissed her, Harry remembered hugging him felt different, horrible and shivery, and too tight. The guard blew a whistle, Daddy climbed on board, and the troop train hissed and spat and lurched away. Now he was somewhere in Italy, listed as missing.

Harry smeared away tears and hauled himself up and out of the cave. He pushed the bushes back so the entrance was hidden again. Up on the dune path he set off for home. The daylight was fading. A flock of gulls flew in perfect V formation towards the steep ridge of rocks at the end of the bay.

'Ack! Ack! Ack!'

A burly boy leapt out of the dunes and pounced. Harry hit out but two more boys brought him down. He landed on the sand with a thud.

'Dead!'

'I'm not dead! Get off!'

'Frank shot you!' cried one of the boys. 'You are dead!'

'And you ain't just missing!' sniggered the other.

14

'What were you doing along there?' demanded Frank Prouse, leering at him.

'Nothing! Get off!'

Frank laughed. 'Nothing! Nothing he says! You appeared pretty quick!'

'We saw you,' nodded Will.

Harry struggled but Ed held his shoulders down and Will's boot was heavy on his ribs. All the local kids knew to do what Frank told them or else, especially these two. The thought of them discovering the cave and Frank lumbering down into it was unbearable. 'I was chasing rabbits.'

Frank sneered. 'Crawling round, looking for rabbits? Pretty stupid! You want to shoot them. Sure it wasn't something for my metal collection?'

'You already took what I had.'

Frank's collection of shrapnel and bullet casings was famous, all frightened out of other kids. Frank glanced back along the path and then grinned. 'Got something to hide from your mother's fancy man, have you?'

That did it! Harry kicked his way up, and launched himself at Frank.

Frank ducked behind the others. 'Come on! Let's sort him out!' he cried, and they all set about him.

Frank's first punch sent Harry reeling. He hit

back but he was no match for three. In all the shouting and pummelling and kicking he was getting the worst of it, and losing. He didn't notice a jeep pull up, and someone racing towards them.

'Whoa! The war's the other side of the Channel!'

With surprising speed Frank was caught by the scruff of the neck. Will was spun away sharply, knocking Ed down, and Harry felt himself pulled up and out of the scrum.

'Get off, GI!' shouted Frank.

'You want to pick on someone your own size,' boomed the GI.

'He started it!'

'Called us names,' said Ed, struggling to his feet.

'I didn't!' Harry protested.

'Did!'

The GI let go and stood between them all. 'There's a mass of fighting around without you kids. And plenty to do.'

Frank straightened up his make-do-and-mend pullover and smirked cheekily. 'Got a sister, mister?'

'Nope! And no gum, chum, neither!'

'What are you doing here, Yank!'

'Stopping the fight, kid!'

'We don't want no Americans here!'

'No?'

They glared at one another in a moment of angry silence.

Then Frank shrugged. 'C'mon,' he said to the other two. He leered at Harry. 'I'll see you later!' He put two fingers up and sauntered off along the path. Ed and Will brushed themselves off and hurried after him.

Harry eyed the soldier suspiciously.

'What were you fighting about? A girl?'

'No!'

'What then?'

'Nothing.'

'Nothing, huh.' The GI looked hard at his eye. 'You're going to have a real shiner!'

Harry's eye was stinging, puffy and tender to touch. He made a face and felt the skin pull.

The GI dug in his pocket and produced two sticks of gum. He held one out and smiled broadly. 'Name's Private Mike White! United States Marines.'

Harry accepted the offering. The silver paper ripped away easily from the grey sugary strip. He folded it into his mouth. Very sweet, even sweeter than the treacle tart his mum used to make. His eye stopped stinging a bit. Chewing enthusiastically, he looked the soldier up and down. There were GIs on the newsreels, but this was his first real one. The boots were far better than British soldiers, all new and polished. Much smarter uniform too. Young looking face, and scrubbed up. A bit of a stupid grin on him, but everyone talked about GIs being as green as new grown grass.

Private Mike White reached over and brushed some of the sand off his jumper. 'I'd stay out of trouble if I were you,' he said.

Harry drew back sharply. 'You one of the GI's coming here?'

'Sure am!' Mike grinned and sauntered off towards his jeep. 'See you around, huh?'

Harry hesitated. Then he followed the GI down to the road. He'd never seen an army jeep close up before. It had mud-spattered wheels and was open-topped and dusty inside. Under an empty coca-cola bottle, a crumpled map of the local coastline hung over the edge of the passenger seat. Harry ran his finger along the bonnet's smooth metal surface.

'Made in America,' said Mike, giving the jeep a friendly slap and leaping nimbly into the driver's seat. 'Hadn't you better be getting home?'

Harry shrugged and glanced nervously along the dunes. It was nearly dark. Frank would be waiting for him up there for sure. He scanned the shoreline instead.

'I got to have a quick look along there.' Mike was pointing at the village.

'What do you GIs want all this for anyway? Why are you here? This is my beach!'

Mike looked at him. 'Your's, huh?'

'That's Torcross. Where I live.'

'Okay.'

'It's mine!'

'So, a lift that way any use to you?'

Harry pressed his finger hard against the jeep's smooth metal. This was a GI, but a lift back was better than the prospect of Frank. It was a long run back along the shoreline. He took a chance and nodded. Mike swept the map and empty bottle off the passenger seat. Harry climbed in. The engine growled and burst into life.

Mike drove slowly, looking out over the bay. The water had that dark steel-grey glittering look of just before darkness. 'Sure is nice here.'

Harry could see Frank and his mates ahead, still on the dunes path. It would be easy to make a cheeky V sign at them as the jeep passed, but then everyone would know he was talking to a

GI. He ducked down.

Mike increased his speed. 'The big guy again, huh?'

'Dropped something.'

'Sure you did.'

Harry pushed his hand into his pocket to make out he really had and sat back up. This jeep had power. No phut-phut-phut engine like the old clapped-out couple of cars round here. And Mike's grip on the wheel was strong, full of energy. No worn out, ripped skin, ground-in-dirt look about his hands. More Americans like him were coming. Harry looked at the beach racing by. Somehow the threat of leaving it was gathering speed.

They pulled up by the post office. It was too dark now to see much of Torcross. There weren't any lights at the windows because of the blackout, just a pale thin line here and there where curtains didn't quite meet.

'Not big, this town, is it?' said Mike, looking across the wide corner where the coast road curled up the hill and inland, then at the shadowy cut-through leading to the beach. He twisted round in his seat to look along the row of seafront houses. And further. 'Nice lagoon.'

'Ley. It's a Ley.'

'A Ley, huh?'

'So what do you want with it? What do you want with any of it? Why come here, GI?'

Mike gazed across at the few cottages tucked in behind the darkening expanse of the Ley. 'My outfit's detailed to help all you folks move out. Here and in Slapton village.' He revved the engine. 'Care to give us a hand?'

'No!' Harry was out of the jeep in a second.

'Look, kid, I'm just following orders.'

'Nobody here wants to leave.'

'But you got to do it.'

'Why?'

'What we need is a little local cooperation.'

'Well, I'm not leaving. My mother cried when she heard.'

A late gull circled slowly over the Ley.

'What's your name, kid?' Harry hesitated. Even his name might be giving too much. But it was just a name.

'Harry Beere.'

Mike grinned. 'Nice to be acquainted, Harry Beere.' He revved the engine, gave a smart salute and drove off.

Harry lingered on the corner. If his mother was still out, the door key would be under the stone. He turned the chewing gum over on his tongue and watched the jeep disappearing into the distance. Usually the coast road was dark. It was years since anyone had dared use headlights.

Chapter Three

Harry was nearly asleep when he heard his mother's voice in the kitchen. Someone else's too. He pushed back the bedclothes and crept to his bedroom door, opening it just a crack.

Mum was taking off her coat. Holding Peppy was Lewis Cramer, the horrible thickset Air Raid Warden who shouted at all the village kids. He'd been here two or three times lately. Harry wanted to run out and snatch Peppy away from him. He wished now he'd minded her. But he waited, watching and listening.

'I have official responsibilities. You're asking a lot of me, Celia.'

'No, no. I just need some advice.'

'Don't you worry your silly little head. I'll come and see you wherever you are.'

She looked up at him nervously. 'But that's just what I mean, Lewis. Where will I be? We don't have family or friends to go to.' Her hair glistened, picking up the lamplight. She took the sleeping Peppy from him and laid her down in her cot.

Lewis took off his helmet and moved in closer.

The keys and chain at his waist jangled. 'Of course I do have influence, Celia. I know a place in Totnes. I can get you in there. You and the little girl.'

'And Harry?'

'Oh, the boy. Yes, and the boy.' Lewis lifted her chin. Harry caught his breath as Lewis's fingers crawled up her face. 'I could drive you there too,' he said. 'Would you like that, Celia?'

Harry saw her hesitate and glance nervously over to his door. She backed away from Lewis and opened the front door. 'Thank you, Lewis.'

Lewis shot an irritated glance towards Harry's bedroom door himself, picked up his helmet and followed. 'Leave it to me, love,' he said. 'They want me to oversee this whole evacuation. I'll make sure you're all right.' He held her face up to his again. 'We could go dancing like the other night. It's good for you to go out. You're a great little dancer.'

Rage rattled through Harry. He wanted to fling his door wide open to shout, 'Don't let him take you out!' But already she'd stepped back and Lewis was gone through the front door. Outside his US jeep roared into life.

Harry slammed his door. How dare she even think of going out with Lewis again! Once was bad enough.

The engine sound faded away. In the moonlit lane outside his window, there were only dark cobblestones. The sour haze of exhaust fumes quickly gave way to clear night air and the familiar smell of salt from the incoming tide.

His bedroom door opened. 'Harry?'

He ignored her.

She came and stood beside him in the moonlight. She saw his eye immediately. 'You've been fighting! Harry!'

He turned away.

'What about?'

'Nothing!'

She put her hand on his shoulder, ready to say something. He shook her off. 'Lewis is a creep!'

'No, he's not.'

'Why do you let him in?'

'Harry, with your father away…'

'Yeah, Daddy's away.'

'We have to have somewhere to go now. Lewis says he can help.' She reached out for the precious photo.

'Don't touch that.' The words fired out of him, spinning like darts at her through the silver moonlight. For a moment he felt her staring at him, then she began picking up his clothes and folding them.

'I need a man to help us now,' she said. 'You can see that, Harry, can't you?'

He turned back to look out at the empty road. He heard her sigh.

'Goodnight,' she said softly, and closed the door behind her.

He flung himself down onto the bed, hating Lewis with every ounce of his being.

Chapter Four

Harry blew on his frozen fingers. Over the road, Lewis was busy exercising his new powers to oversee the evacuation. 'Don't argue with me, woman! I'm saying there'll be no more fil-im shows in the village hall. I make the rules now!'

'It's several days till most people go, Mr Cramer. What they need is cheering up, not rules.'

'I'll have the door sealed.'

'You will not!'

'These people are required to pack their belongings and vacate this area. Anything which distracts them is unlawful. Requisition has already taken effect, and the Admiralty may at any time and without notice enforce their right to immediate possession.'

'Oh stop quoting at me, you silly little man!' said Miss Markham, shutting her post office door.

'No fil-ims! By order!' Lewis shouted angrily. He took out his black notebook and wrote something down. Two women hurrying past Harry whispered to each other. 'How dare he? After all the things she does to get precious letters out to our men?'

But Lewis was already striding off to pick on other people. Harry's friend Tim, his father and his little sister Lillie were in the firing line now. Lewis jabbed a finger to his watch. 'Why aren't you at work, Jed Trow? There's fields to be cleared, and the deadline's looming.'

'It's Sunday, sir,' said Jed, respectfully lifting his cap. Tim's eyebrows rose. Nobody in the village liked Lewis, and little Lillie was really afraid of him. 'He's got nasty owl eyes,' she said. Now, her eyes focussed firmly on her father, and she clung on tight to his hand. Wrapped up in shabby grey woollies, she looked like a scrappy baby sparrow in a nest, terrified of being snatched. Looking at Lewis, Harry bet his own little sister would feel the same. And Peppy was smaller, easier to snatch. He caught Tim's eye and pulled a face.

'Where's their gas masks?' demanded Lewis, opening his black book again. Tim turned his back on Lewis to show his, taking the chance to grin over at Harry.

Jed had Lillie's. 'I've worked this land all me life, Mr Cramer,' he said. 'My cottage is tied. What do me and the children do now?'

'You move like the rest,' said Lewis.

'But we don't have nowhere to go.'

28

'Stop moaning, Jed Trow. Don't you know there's a war on?'

Jed hung his head, and pulled his thin worn jacket closer against the biting cold. 'I promised me wife when she died I'd keep the little ones with me.'

But Lewis was looking past Jed to a GI jeep arriving.

'If you can't cooperate,' he said, 'I'll report you to the higher authorities and those kids will be taken off you.'

Clinging to Lillie's hand, Jed hurried away up the hill. Lewis straightened his helmet and headed for the jeep.

Tim scooted over to Harry. 'Creep!'

'Who put him in charge?' whispered Harry.

'Who says he is?' said Tim, pulling on his gas mask. 'Cock a doodle do?' Harry stifled a giggle and nodded. They both breathed out inside their masks. Gentle raspberry noises warmed them up, then at Tim's signal they both blew hard. Lewis heard the glorious eruption and turned back scowling. The GIs in the jeep laughed. Lewis strode back and cuffed Harry roughly round the ear.

'Ow!'

'Don't you get in my way, boy,' he hissed. 'You

hear?'

Harry tore off his mask and clutched his throbbing ear. 'We're practising,' he protested, as Tim let out another blast. Lewis cuffed him even harder and strode off towards the jeep again. Tim pulled off his mask. His ear was crimson. He held his fingers up in an angry V sign to Lewis's back.

'What's holding you up, Warden?' one of the GIs called.

'I'm not having these disruptive youngsters questioning my authority!' Lewis shouted back. 'I'm in charge here.'

'Would the GIs care if he beat us up?' whispered Tim as Lewis strode off towards them. 'They just want us out.' He rubbed his ear. 'Where did you get the black eye?'

Harry shrugged. 'Come on,' he said, aching to run on the shore and feel free.

It was dark when he sprinted home, starving hungry, skin tingling, and lungs raw with the icy winter air. He burst in the front door, breathless. His mother froze, staring at him as if he was a ghost.

'What?'

'Heavens, you're so like your father. For a moment...' She brushed her hair away quickly from her forehead. Now she was looking at him properly, that look she often used, challenging him to speak up and say where he'd been.

He wanted to smile at her, and say I know I've been out too long and not helping you, Mum, sorry, but Tim and I had this fantastic Bomber Command game on the beach, war planes, and you should have seen how fast we ran. And we climbed on the boats, and the tide was in and the rock pools were full of those little tiny pink crabs all crawly and see-through and one day I'll take Peppy down there and she can poke them with her finger but I promise I won't let her get nipped and… and gosh, what you're cooking smells wonderful, and I love coming home and finding you here all warm and…

'Jed's been here,' she said, tipping chopped carrot into the big pot steaming on the stove. 'He's in trouble for not working today. All the fields have to be cleared. They're desperate up there. I promised you'd help him for me tomorrow.'

Harry flopped down onto the old sofa, exhausted. 'Why do we have to leave, Mum?'

'Ssh! Don't wake Peppy. I've just got her off.'
Peppy was curled up in her cot, looking like a

tiny sea snail, hugging her woolly blanket, doing that little puffy breathing she did when she dreamed. Clutched in her fingers was a long gull feather he'd found on the dunes.

'What about school?'

'No school. They don't want people gathering. Anyway the school's packing up too.'

He wished his mother would come over and give him a comforting hug like she used to. Look at the bruise under his eye. Say how purple-y dark it was, how fast it was coming out. He wanted to hear that funny laugh of hers that always made him feel like laughing too. But she was over there by the stove, and he was here, and somehow there was too much space between. Since Daddy went to war, this room seemed big and empty. He wished he could build a bridge, run over it and get to the other side, to her stove side, quick.

Instead he could feel her seeing the layers of grit and sand from the beach crumbling off his clothes onto her clean sofa. 'Look at you!' she cried. 'There can't be a good reason to come home like that!'

'Mum?'

Over on the stove where she was the kettle was coming to the boil.

'When Daddy comes home, what if we're not here?'

She reached for the teapot. 'You could have been here helping me pack things up. One good thing, Lewis will take us in his car.' She poured the boiling water into the pot. 'You look cold.'

Before she could turn round again he was shutting his bedroom door against her.

'There'll be soup later,' she called. 'Harry?'

He didn't answer.

She was just on the other side of the door. 'Harry?'

He heard her move away. The wireless was on now and he could smell the cooked soup. He opened the door a crack. Peppy was fast asleep. His mother was curled up on the sofa by the wireless. He wondered if she might be crying. He wanted to go out there and sit beside her and listen with her like Daddy used to, so she wouldn't be by herself. Instead he took the bowl of soup from the floor beside his door and pulled back inside. He sat on his bed eating it. It was warm and delicious and comforting. Afterwards he lay on the bed watching the shadows on the wall in the lamp light and looking at the photograph.

He could hear the hum of the wireless and Mr

Churchill was saying:

We did not undertake this task because we had counted the cost, or because we had carefully measured the duration. We took it on because duty and honour called us to it, content to drive on until we have finished the job.

Chapter Five

Frost laced the leaves of the hedge together. Streams of water often ran off the high bank into the lane. Today long fingers of ice hung there instead. Harry pulled his old wool scarf closer.

He could hear the rhythmic throb and chew of the threshing machine grinding the thin corn stukes from this late harvest. The dawn air was a mixture of chugging steam, fresh turned earth, and dank winter cold. Through a gap in the hedge he could see women pitch-forking, and limp hay showering onto their wagon. Anybody would see the hay was too damp, but the women still bent and pitched, bent and pitched.

Further up the lane Jed's tractor was purring. Harry climbed the top field gate and balanced. Gulls were flying over the tractor as if it was a fishing boat. Dickie, a boy from school, Dickie's father, and two other men, the only farm hands left apart from Jed, followed it too, all of them walking in furrows of red earth churned up by the plough, gathering up from the ground instead of planting into it.

'Come on, lad,' bellowed Jed. 'Stop dreaming.'

Harry jumped down into the field, pleased to see Tim was there as well. The farm dogs bounded over, barking an enthusiastic welcome and sniffing affectionately at his heels. He took the sack Tim thrust at him, joined the line, and began the hard work of bending to pick up hardly grown scrawny carrots.

'Where's your mother?' asked Tim.

'She's packing. Sorting. Doing washing and stuff. I'm stuck with chasing Peppy round.'

There was momentary halt as Jed jumped down from the tractor to clear one of the blades. He picked up a carrot. 'Too much of a gamble,' he said angrily, throwing it aside. 'And where's the new ground for them, I want to know?' He looked exhausted as he climbed back up.

'But they're our carrots,' muttered one of the men, picking it up.

Tim frowned. 'Been working all night, my dad has,' he said, as they followed again. 'Says he might as well. He can't sleep. The Warden reported him yesterday.'

'Why?'

'For not working Sundays.'

Cold red mud stuck to Harry's fingers, and to his arms too. He felt it squish into the holes in his shoes, and splatter cold up his long socks. It stuck to his freezing bare knees and clung to the frayed edges of his short trousers. Soon his jumper was covered in it too. Tim chucked more at him. And Dickie Holme tried it. Irritated, Harry took careful aim with a carrot and caught Tim right on the ear just as Jed looked round.

'Keep up, Dickie,' Jed called, angrily. 'There's no time for silly games.'

Dickie glared at Harry and moved away.

Tim laughed. 'Good shot!'

'No school then?'

'Every cloud has a silver lining. It could be great, this leaving, you know. A real adventure!' There was a roar from the tractor engine as Jed accelerated, forcing the pace. What there was of morning sun warmed the field earth and made it steam.

'What do the GIs want with our land?' Harry complained as they reached the top of the field. 'Why do we have to go?'

'Dad says they're going to play at killing each other,' said Tim. Harry stared at him. The gulls rose high and circled, waiting.

'General Eisenhower was here. That's what old Mitchelmay reckons. Nobody believes him, but he swears they're up to something. There'll be an invasion here maybe. Lewis warned him to keep his mouth shut. Careless words cost lives and all that.' The tractor began turning to go down the field again.

'Come on,' shouted Jed.

'Know where you're heading?'

Harry shrugged. He wasn't going to tell Tim the Warden would have anything to do with where they might go. 'You?'

Tim shook his head. 'Nowhere yet. The GIs came this morning to pack us up. Dad didn't want to be there and he farmed Lillie out last night so she wouldn't get upset. The GIs offered me candy! Trying to bribe me to stay and help.'

'Did you?'

'I took the sweets! But not in front of my dad. And then I told them I couldn't stay. I had to slave in the fields 'cos of them.'

Harry thought of the good chewing gum and the GI jeep ride. He screwed up his nose to see if the skin round his eye still hurt. It did a bit. He picked up a missed carrot, rubbed the earth off it and looked out across the field. From up here there was a clear view of Start Bay, the sweeping curve of the beach and the coast road, with the Ley curling along behind it. A burst of morning sunlight suddenly clipped the edge of the clouds and lit everything up. The sea glittered. The Ley shone. His bay, his beach, his hide in the sand dunes.

'What's that?' he asked, looking across to vehicles and men moving around on the hill above Torcross.

'Accommodation camp,' Tim said. 'The Yanks are already making themselves at home.'

Peppy stopped climbing over him and picked at the loose thread round a hole in his jumper. Harry pulled her busy little fingers off and grabbed at her bare toes. 'This little piggy went to market, this little piggy stayed home...' She twisted away from him, giggling.

'Mum?' he said. 'Jed thinks the GIs want our land to play killing games.'

She looked up from the ironing, shocked. 'I've never heard such rubbish. Jed's cross because he's in trouble.'

'Why are they here then?'

'To help us win this awful war, of course. So we can finish with fighting.'

'Farmer Mitchelmay says he saw General Eisenhower.'

'Here? Never!'

'Michelmay thinks there's going to be an

invasion. Is Hitler coming?'

There was a yelp of panic, the smell of singe. His mother snatched the hot iron up off the pillowcase, as if she might cry. 'Now look what you made me do!'

Chapter Six

A jeep drove past. It was Harry's GI.

'Look! Truckloads of them,' said Tim, pointing to another US army vehicle heading in along the coast road, 'I hate them.'

Harry kicked a stray pebble. 'Maybe they're only following orders.'

'You a sympathiser?'

'No!'

Lewis was over by the village hall. The GI with him was hammering a board across the entrance door.

'Look at the Warden,' said Tim. 'Can't wait to stop us doing things.' Bang... bang... bang. The sound swirled around in Harry's head. 'What difference can it make to the GIs if we watch the newsreels? It's pictures of them!'

Tim nodded. 'Mean old beggar, Lewis is.'

'Clear off you kids!' the Warden shouted. Lilly hid behind Tim as Lewis ran past chasing other children.

Harry shoved his clenched fists inside his pockets. 'Come on. Let's go!'

Tim shook his head. 'Got to take Lillie back.

And fetch water. And then see what I can find for her to eat. If there is anything. The GIs boxed us up well and truly.'

Old Reg Thompson waved to Harry from behind some boxes. 'Your mother and Peppy all right?' he called. 'Wish your dad was here to give us all a hand.'

Harry nodded. He should go home and help, he knew it, but leaving while Daddy was away didn't feel right. Other kids were helping their mums. Lifting and carrying. Dragging sacks of dug-up vegetables. Squeezing easy chairs and beds out through narrow front doors. Struggling on the other end of cupboards. Family belongings were stacked on paths, labelled, but no-one spoke to the teams of GIs packing it all onto their trucks.

Somewhere Lewis was barking orders. Behind a tall Victorian dresser smelling of log fires and spice, Harry heard Miss Markham's voice. 'How dare he! Keeping those children out of that hall. Reporting me! For four years I've waved the flag and collected for the war effort. Spitfires. Ships. Guns. We've all made do and mended. Worked harder and longer. Now suddenly we have to move out of our village to make way for Americans, and that little Hitler's allowed to make his petty rules and push people about.'

'It's government orders,' said Mary Hayton, stroking her old dog.

'He's the Warden. What choice have we got?'

'The last one was a dear old chap. '

'There's talk of an attack,' said Amy Wardle, hurrying by. 'We should be glad the Americans are over here.'

Down by the Ley, in the tiny front garden of his end-of-terrace cottage, Abraham Thorn, his thin white hair awry, leaned on his stick and watched the activity.

'Come to help in the garden again?' he grunted when Harry reached him. 'Dig for victory and all that rubbish?' No whiskery old smile and pleasure on his face today.

There didn't seem much point to weeding and watering with him if his garden was about to be abandoned. 'A GI asked me to help them,' Harry confessed. 'Co-operate with the evacuation.'

Old Mr Thorn glanced at him, then pulled his dusty old winter coat collar up round his ears, and watched Lewis along by the post office ordering people about. He shook his head and leaned towards a late rose doing its best to bloom in the winter air. The skin on his hand as he held it looked like crumpled paper. The pink petals brushed his wrinkled lips as he slowly breathed in its sweetness. 'Could be the last rose ever,' he said.

'Last?' said Harry. 'Not the last.'

The old man nodded. 'Tis.' His beady old eyes followed two GIs with rifles slung over their shoulders knocking loudly on the cottage door at the far end of the terrace. 'It feels like invasion, does this,' he muttered. 'Booting us all out.'

A sudden screech and fumes burst into Harry's throat.

'Mind the boy!' screamed old Mr Thorn. A US jeep halted a hair's breadth from Harry, pressing him hard against the cottage stone wall.

Old Mr Thorn shot out a trembling hand to him. 'All right, lad?'

Harry nodded. Shivering inside with shock, he squeezed free. Unashamed the young GI driving the jeep backed up and buzzed on. 'Invasion,' yelled the old man after him.

'It's only the Yanks, Mr Thorn,' Harry said bravely, but he could feel his voice shaking. He dusted himself down to feel calmer.

'Ha!' Abraham Thorn's pale whiskery cheeks drew in and blew out again as the US jeep sped away along the Ley lane. 'Foreign powers!' he snorted. 'They'll bring their ways with them and we'll never be shot of 'em.' He glanced past Harry suddenly, and retreated inside.

'I'll come in the morning, shall I? Help you?' Harry asked, but the cottage door closed. He turned round to find Lewis writing in his horrid black book.

In the Cut leading through to the beach the lame fisherman was winding up all his nets. Lobster baskets and crab pots were stacked ready to go.

'Everybody's leaving, Albert,' Harry said.

'Got to,' said Albert. 'Can't go out in the bay no more from 'ere.'

'Why do the GIs want our village?'

'Could be trouble coming and they're not telling us.'

'An invasion?'

Albert shrugged. 'Could be.'

Harry took the worn rope Albert held out. The plaiting bit into his hands as the fisherman pulled on it, tying the rest of the net up together. 'Where will you go?'

'Reckon I'll use what's left of me sea legs and head for the high seas.'

'What, the Navy?'

'Merchant Navy if they'll have me, aye.' Albert slung the nets over his shoulder, picked up baskets and a lobster pot. 'They need men for them Atlantic convoys.'

'But there's U boats!'

Albert headed for the cart. 'No enemy torpedo will get me!'

Harry seized more baskets and followed.

'Won't be able to play round my boat no more, you 'n your friend,' said Albert.

'No,' Harry said, thinking back to the time he'd spent on the beach helping Dad repair Albert's boat. And the spitting sparks from the forge fire and the rhythmic clang as Dad heated and hammered the old metal rowlocks back into shape. Mending the boat was the last thing they'd done together.

'No more fishing for sand eels neither.'

'Where is the boat?'

'She's on the mud round at Kingsbridge. Got no use for 'er here now. Nor for me.'

It took time to load the cart. The cobbles were paler where the pots and baskets had been, their shapes still there like ghosts.

'Heard from your father?' asked Albert.

'No.'

'Missing might just mean he's a prisoner of war.'

'When they let him out and he comes back,

Albert, how will he find us?'

Albert's grey eyes clouded over as he glanced back towards the beach. 'T'was his home, this shore. Don't you forget that.' He patted Harry's shoulder affectionately. 'You and your mother be all right?'

Harry nodded, though being all right was the last thing he was sure of. He watched Albert pick up the wooden handles of his cart and haul his old way of life slowly up the hill. 'See you soon?' he called after him.

Through a blur of stupid tears he looked along the coast road. GIs were helping people load things into army trucks.

Along by the Ley, Lewis and a British army official stood together on an army truck shouting out information. 'Every person should be gone as soon as possible. The supply of electricity will cease, and so will the present arrangements for supplying food…'

Near them Mary Hayton, in WVS uniform now, was demonstrating how to tie up household belongings in a bed sheet. There were sheets like that at home.

A US jeep pulled up out by old Mr Thorn's house. To pack him up?

'Want one?' Freddie Tapler grinned at Harry

and held out a cardboard box. His little brother George was about to disappear round the corner loaded up with more. 'Quick!'

Harry shook his head fast and ducked away. His mother might need boxes but the dreaded Mrs Prouse was heading for them. 'Here!' she screamed, clouting Freddie and snatching the boxes his brother George had. She hit out at them with a grubby potato sack. George grabbed it away and danced round her. 'Ow!' she shrieked, 'Give it here!' She seized her broom. Both boys ran for their lives. 'When I'm gone you can all have whatever's left!' she announced breathlessly to anyone who might be listening. 'But while I'm still here…' She stood, broomstick in hand, glowering, daring anyone to help themselves without her permission.

She sighted Harry. 'And you! You can stop attacking my Frank!' she shouted. 'Fighting yesterday! Jumping on him in the dunes! I've reported you to the Warden. You wait! He'll be after you. You should be ashamed!'

'Cow!'

Harry turned to see Tim grinning at him. 'There's an auction up at Mitchelmay's farm. Coming?'

Chapter Seven

Mitchelmay's cattle pressed hide to quivering hide, their milky breath steaming on the air. Their long discordant moans were like notes on the church organ. Harry and Tim squeezed past the heaving herd. Maybe they're singing, Harry thought, running his hand along a smooth white and honey-coloured rump. Singing to remind them of what they were leaving behind; early spring mornings in the fields above Slapton Sands, fresh pasture, barns full of sweet warm hay. It would be the sounds of the beach in his head if he left. In his dad's too, he was sure.

'Wake up, Harry!' called Tim, clambering up onto an old splintered cart for a view of it all. 'Stop dreaming!'

Harry hauled himself up.

All the local farmers were here, wrapped up against the cold, and strangers too, men in dark suits. Across the smell of fur and dung, the auctioneer began, a monotonous jabbering, another strange droning song.

'Those people know a bargain when they see one,' said Tim. 'The farmers are losing so much money.'

'I can't understand. The words are so fast,' Harry said.

'Every lot's going lower because old Mitchelmay has to sell. He was threatened they'd take his land before the deadline.'

'Why?'

'You know!' Tim whispered. 'The invasion. Ssh!'

Prices fell further. It was mostly the dark suits bidding, and bidding low. 'Who are they?' whispered Harry.

'Know what breed these cows are?' asked Tim, ignoring his question. Harry didn't. 'South Devon, of course. All local, they are. And know what you get if you sit under them?'

Harry frowned and shook his head again.

Tim's face screwed up. 'A pat on the head.'

They both exploded with giggles. Harry nudged him. 'Ssh! It's serious.' But Tim was doubled over, clutching his middle, almost crying with laughter. 'Ssh!' he echoed, taking deep breaths to recover. 'Ssh! It's serious!'

Near them, Mr Mitchelmay looked tearful. All the fields above Slapton were his. The farmer beside him shook his head in sympathy. 'Careless words, eh? Now we can't give the beggars away.'

Prices tumbled further. 'Those who stood by Mitchelmay are selling too,' Tim whispered. 'That's the trouble.'

'To other farms?'

'For slaughter of course.'

Harry's stomach turned over. 'Killing?' He jumped down from the cart.

Tim looked down at him. 'Come on. They die anyway. You can't move a whole herd without having somewhere to go. At least this way they won't need feeding. There is a war on, you know.'

Harry strode away towards the barns.

Tim ran to catch up with him. 'GIs said to stay a few more days in our cottage. Too little to load so they don't want to bother. And we don't know if Dad will get work yet. What kind. Or where.'

The auction was over but people stayed, whispering in huddled groups. A makeshift desk was set up in the barn with a big handwritten sign: Agricultural Committee. Farm workers were giving their names to find new work inland. Jed joined the queue, thrusting Lillie at the boys. She leaned nervously against Harry, reaching up for his hand like Peppy.

'The Warden made her cry last night,' said

Tim. 'Shouted at her about being out late when she was only waiting in the lane for our dad to come home.'

Harry looked down at Lillie. Her hair wasn't brushed and her torn woolly scarf was wrapped round her chin and right up over her mouth. She was such a tiny little thing. He boiled at the thought of the warden shouting at her. If Lewis dared shout at Peppy he'd…

'Listen,' said Tim.

Jed reached the desk. 'Jed Taylor. Worked all me life with cows. And planting. And harvest. Sheep. I can do shearing.'

'But not on Sundays we hear.' Both committee men began to fill in forms.

'Lewis!' whispered Tim.

'And there's me kids.' Jed pointed over. 'I'll do anything, anything,' he pleaded.

One of the committee men beckoned.

'We're wanted.' Tim grabbed Lillie's hand and headed off towards his dad.

Out in the yard a lorry was loaded with cattle. Harry ran his hand along the slats. The cows looked out at him with mournful brown eyes, eagerly licking his fingers with their hot wet tongues.

Nearby two farmers shook hands on a deal. 'Not much time left to save anything now,' one said.

'I'll bring my flock up to you this week. Better summit for them dear old ewes than slaughter.'

'Poor Mitchelmay. Ruined. Should have kept his suspicions to himself. You reckon it really was Eisenhower?'

The other lowered his voice. 'Something's up. Why would the Supreme Allied Commander come here?'

'Ssh! Over by the lorry.'

'That's the blacksmith's boy.'

'He's been talking to GIs, that one. Listed missing, his father is.' And they turned away so Harry couldn't hear what else they said.

A US jeep was parked in the yard. Silver. Dusty wheels. Cola bottle. Map. Behind him Harry heard the rattle of the farm lorry engine, revving up. It rumbled slowly out the gate. Low moan notes hung on the air. The Devon cows were singing.

Chapter Eight

'Harry?' His mum waved frantically from the early morning queue outside the butcher's. Peppy was with her.

Nearer, in another agitated queue by the Post Office, a woman was sobbing and he could hear Miss Markham's voice: 'Not to worry. You'll get your money. Everything will be all right. Just you go to your local Post Office when you get there…'

'Some of us don't know where we'll be.'

Miss Markham's answer was firm. 'Wherever you go.'

In the other direction by the beachfront houses, GIs were loading goods and furniture onto US lorries.

His mum waved again. Harry leaned down and pulled up his socks. At home by the fire steaming washing dripped onto the lino. The piles of ironing grew, and the piles of packing. Potatoes needed digging out of the ground to put in sacks to take. The water buckets needed filling. Peppy was being naughty, hiding, crying, getting into everything. Worst of all, Daddy's things were being left in the cupboards. 'Stop fussing,

Harry,' was all Mum said. 'Six months they say it is. Nine maybe. We can't take everything.'

Will and Ed were down by the butchers too, sitting on the stone wall, swinging their legs excitedly. Leaving home was all adventure to them. An official looking car pulled slowly away from the corner shop. It was packed with possessions with Mrs Prouse sitting up in front next to the driver, staring straight ahead, eyes red. In the back seat, next to his skinny little brother Bill, Frank had a much more familiar expression. Harry ducked down and took advantage of the cover of the car to run until he was out of his mum's sight. And out of breath too. The car speeded up and left him behind, heading out onto the coast road. Frank glared back through the rear window. Here at last was the chance! Harry lifted his fingers and made a cheeky V sign.

When he looked around he was right by Mrs Gale's, the end house in the beach terrace. Mike and two other GIs were loading her belongings onto an army truck. They were lifting and stacking, and wrapping old blankets round her bits and bobs of furniture.

As Harry watched, Mrs Gale came out her door with another box. She added it to the pile and stood staring at it. The bright red wool of her jumper clung to her curvy figure and made her pretty blonde hair look even fairer.

Mike saw him. 'Thought you weren't coming, Harry Beere,' he called, heading for the boxes.

'I'm not.' Past Mrs Gale's was only a different way onto the beach.

As he wondered how best to walk on by, Mike picked up the top box and suddenly Mrs Gale seemed to lose her wits. She screamed and wrenched the box back. What on earth was wrong with her? She glared at Mike accusingly. 'It's my husband,' she cried.

'Sure, ma'm. Sure it is.'

She was hugging the box, and swaying on her feet, in some sort of trance. Mike offered his hand. She shrank away. The other GIs glanced at each other nervously. 'He's in every box,' she cried. 'You can't have him!'

Mrs Gale had been on the station saying goodbye to Mr Gale the same day Daddy left. Pale and crying then. Right on the edge of tears now. Harry hurried over and took her arm to steady her. 'Where are you going with him, Mrs Gale?'

Mrs Gale blinked.

'Where are you going with him?' he repeated.

'Harry,' she said, looking at him blankly.

'Want me to carry that?' he asked.

She looked down at the box in her arms. 'It's all his things. Our wedding picture.'

He nodded. 'I've got a special photograph of my dad too.' He reached out. 'Shall I carry the box? I promise I'll be really careful.' A moment passed, but then Mrs Gale passed the box over. Harry accepted it as if it contained pure gold. Now he had it, the only place to take it was round to the back of the truck. 'Mr Gale is in the army,' he whispered to the GI there. 'He's away fighting.'

He went back to Mrs Gale who was sitting on one of the other boxes. She was trembling. He sat down next to her and put his arm round her shoulder to comfort her. She smelt of some pretty flower scent. 'You mustn't worry,' he said. 'They know everything's really important.'

'It's all I got of him,' she said miserably.

'Where is he?'

Mrs Gale pushed her blonde hair back from her face and looked at him for a moment before she answered. Her expression calmed as if she suddenly recognised who he was. 'Safe,' she said quietly, and stood up.

Mike came over and smiled kindly at her. 'Are

you going far, ma'm?'

Mrs Gale took a deep, steadying breath. 'To my sister in Derby. I don't get on with her, but...' Her conversation sounded normal again. 'Well, we have to go, don't we?'

Harry turned on Mike. 'Why? Why do we have to go?'

'Harry, it's all right. It's not his fault.' The smile Mrs Gale gave Mike was forced and watery. 'All these things are for the station.'

'That'll be just fine, m'am.' Mike picked up another box. 'Could you stay just now?' he whispered to Harry. 'As she knows you?'

Harry glanced nervously back along the road to see who was watching. It wasn't as if he would be helping GIs. He was helping Mrs Gale. And Peter Gale was Daddy's best friend. Daddy would help. He chose a small box and took it to the truck.

'How will she manage on the train?' he asked Mike, when Mrs Gale went indoors.

Mike shook his head. 'She seems to have some plan for further up the line.'

When her belongings were all stacked on the truck, one of the GIs climbed into the driving seat. Mrs Gale locked her front door tearfully and put the key in her handbag. She saw Harry looking at her. 'You take care,' she said, pulling on her coat, and buttoning it up.

'Here,' Mike whispered to him when she was climbing into the truck. 'Give her this.'

'Twenty dollars?' She stared at the money in total amazement.

'The GI thought you might need it.'

'I can't…'

'Sure you can,' said Mike.

She looked back at them all gratefully. 'Thank you.'

Chapter Nine

'It's real tough moving out of your own home town,' Mike said.

'Everyone's really angry. Nobody wants to go.'

'It's hard for them to understand we only want to help.'

'They all hate you. I'll be hated for talking to you.'

Mike squinted along the row of houses. 'I was in school when I was drafted. I had a life.'

Harry stared at him. 'School? Don't you know anything?'

Mike laughed. 'A year into local agricultural college, kid. I want to work on the land.'

'You have to go to school for that?'

'Yep. If you're going to do prairie farming and grow things real good, you need to know what you're talking about.' A flock of gulls rose up screaming from beach. Mike watched them fly inland over the hill fields. 'I guess I'm seeing some different country over here.'

An empty truck arrived and parked further along. The other GI went to speak to the driver. Mike turned back to Harry. 'You know all these folks, don't you, kid?'

Harry drew back. 'Talk to Miss Markham,' he said. 'She's the post office lady.' He pointed to her place. 'She organises everyone.'

'So it's not that ugly Warden guy?'

Harry giggled. 'No. Not the ugly Warden guy!' He kicked a pebble into the gutter. 'Old Mr Thorn says he'll only leave here in a wooden box.'

'Which one's Mr Thorn?'

Harry pointed across the Ley. 'End cottage. I help him in his garden.'

'That very old guy.'

'We dig for victory.'

'You do?'

'My dad used to help him.'

'Where is your dad right now?'

'Don't know.'

Mike glanced at him.

Harry kicked at another loose stone. 'Italy somewhere. Fighting.'

'Hey, bud?' called the other GIs. 'We got a job to do.'

Mike sighed. 'Growing stuff is real good.' He set off towards the truck.

Harry hesitated and then followed. 'Old Mr Thorn showed me how to take cuttings. He says vegetables grow just as well as flowers.'

'So how old is this Thorn guy?'

'Nearly eighty!'

'Wow! A lifetime's experience! You sure got yourself a good agricultural teacher there.' Mike looked up at the next house in the terrace.

'Miss Bland,' Harry offered. 'She works the telephone exchange. Her name's Kathleen.'

Miss Bland looked hard at Harry when he knocked. 'You're not helping them?' she demanded. 'Harry!'

'I was making sure Mrs Gale was all right,' he whispered. 'And they were ever so nice to her.'

Miss Bland looked past him to the truck.

He nodded earnestly. 'Really kind.'

Mike came up the path. 'Hi there, Kathleen. Can we help you at all?' His wide smile seemed to impress her, and when Harry nodded encouragingly, it was surprising how quickly she was showing what needed moving.

'Think you might care to hang on here a little while?' Mike asked him. 'Seeing as she knows you?'

Maybe a few more minutes wouldn't matter.

It took all four of them, Harry, Mike and two GIs to move Kathleen's precious sideboard out of her house. 'It was my mother's. I can't leave it behind

62

though God knows where I'm going to put it!' When they finally heaved it up on to the truck, Kathleen made them some tea, and ran along to the WVS for some sandwiches. They sat on her dining chairs to eat them. Harry couldn't believe how the GIs screwed up their noses at the potted meat filling. Mike persevered but the other two went off to find something else.

'Thanks for talking to me,' Mike.

Harry looked up from another hungry bite. 'Hmm?'

'Nobody else does.'

Harry thought what else he could say. 'Old Mr Thorn's got a bomb shelter. See that slope behind his cottage?' He pointed across the Ley again. 'My dad terraced all that. And they made the best vegetable garden in the village. The shelter's at the top. It's a shed really but it's dug back into the earth. There's a corrugated iron roof like the real Anderson shelters. Old Mr Thorn and I covered that over with earth too.'

'You and your dad sure have helped the old guy.'

Harry shrugged. 'No point now.' He wolfed down the last of his sandwich. 'Have you seen the curlews?'

'Curlews?'

'Birds. They're my dad's favourite.'

'Back home in the mid west you see buzzards. Old carrion birds. Huge. Winging round in the sky, hour after hour.'

'Curlews have this wonderful call. It's like bubbling sort of echo over the water. Old Mr Thorn and I have tea up in the shelter and watch them feeding. It's a good view from there.'

'Tea, huh?' said Mike, abandoning his last sandwich onto Harry's empty plate and digging into his pocket. 'All I've got is chewing gum and candy.'

Chapter Ten

Harry took Peppy's little finger and traced it over his best piece of shiny slate. 'It's like the water's edge.' The ridges dipped into the surface like rippling seawater, as if this one stone might contain the whole history of tides. 'There's slate on our beach everywhere. I'm going to show this to Mike.'

'Mmm.' Peppy snuggled in closer to him, away from the high pile of ironing beside her. 'Mummy?'

He put the slate down and reached into his pocket. 'Here, I got you candy.' He un-wrapped the boiled sweet. Peppy turned it round and round in her fingers, delighted by its bright ruby colour. 'No! Eat it, sticky fingers!' He took it back and popped it in her mouth. 'Quick, before Mummy comes home.' She looked up at him, sucking hard and fast. Her blue eyes were like the glittery shallows of the bay.

He poked her middle and grinned. 'What would you do without your big brother, eh?'

Next morning he was up and out long before his

mother woke. The dawn air was icy. He did up more buttons on his jacket and thrust his hands deeper into his pockets. The slate stone weighed one side down and was cold to touch, but he pushed his fingers past it anyway. He wondered if Tim might be hanging round, but there was no sign of him. More than likely he'd be working up in the fields with his dad again, getting covered in sticky, freezing red mud. Helping the GIs was a lot warmer than that, and surprisingly more cheerful.

On the corner, Mrs Green's sons were carrying furniture out of her guesthouse. She was cleaning her windows. 'You're a little turncoat,' she hissed down from her ladder. 'Fancy helping them throw us out!' Shocked, Harry ducked his head down and hurried on. Around in the Ley lane he could see Miss Markham banging on old Mr Thorn's door. There was no point going there. The time for gardening was gone. Mist was drifting across the Ley again. If Mike wanted to see a curlew, there might be some there now feeding in the shallows. Maybe they could walk over together and see.

His three GIs were closer to the shops today, their truck parked halfway along the row of seafront houses. But people like Mrs Green weren't waiting for their assistance. There was already plenty of furniture out all along the street.

Mike smiled broadly when he saw him. 'Hey! The kid's here, guys.' The other GIs grinned. Mike held out a brown paper bag. 'Great you could come. Better start the day right!'

Inside the bag was a fresh sugary doughnut. First bite, delicious fruity jam burst into Harry's mouth.

'I looked out for a curlew this morning,' Mike said watching him enjoying the doughnut. 'But no dice.'

Harry licked his lips and looked up the house beside them. 'Amy Wardle's father-in-law lives here. Amy plays the church organ.'

'Where's the church?'

Harry pointed a sticky finger along to Slapton. 'See the spire?'

'The one by the Chantry, huh?'

The upstairs window opened, and old Mr Wardle looked down at them all. He was still in his pyjamas. 'I'm up. I am up. Stop chasing me. My daughter-in-law will be along in a minute.'

'That's okay, Mr Wardle,' Mike called. 'We'll wait for Amy. I promise we won't chase you. You take your time.'

Harry pulled the slate out of his pocket. 'I

brought this to show you.' He watched Mike stroke the surface. 'It's everywhere on this beach.'

Mike looked out along the coast. 'It's like all those waves in the bay are cut into it.'

Harry licked the last of the jam off his fingers. 'Here comes Amy.'

Amy wasn't pleased to see them but she ushered them all inside to see what was what. 'Tell your mum,' she said to Harry, 'tell her I'll have to see her when I see her. There's my place to do as well as here.'

Old Mr Wardle leaned over the landing. 'What about me chickens, Amy?' He struggled down the stairs and looked around in confusion. 'Won't find a thing I own ever again,' he said. 'Always know where things are here. You live in a place all your life and you know where things are.'

Amy gave him a hug. 'Don't worry, my old duck,' she said. 'I'll make you some tea.'

They began piling boxes Amy had already packed out by the truck.

'Private White?' Further down the road Miss Markham waved urgently.

'It's the organising lady,' said Mike.

'Private White?' She hurried along towards them.

'How come they all know your name, White?'

asked one of the other GIs.

Mike winked at Harry. 'I must talk to the right people,' he said.

'We don't have much time,' Miss Markham said, arriving breathless. 'Could you possibly give me a hand, do you think?'

Mike looked mystified. 'Me, Ma'm?'

'You told me you want to help. And this is important. Come on.'

Mike glanced at the others and raised his eyebrows. He set off after Miss Markham.

'He was officially warned,' Harry heard her say. 'They threatened him!' Curious, he dumped the box he had on the pile and followed.

'Heart,' Miss Markham said, as she led the way urgently through the clutter of furniture and carts. 'And Bishop's still up at the church.'

The corner ahead was crowded. A queue used up one side, a long steam engine of people, breathing white mist into the cold air, all keen for hot cups of WVS tea. On the other side was all Mrs Green's furniture, sideboards, boxes, dining tables, bedsteads, tied bundles of bedding. As Miss Markham and Mike headed through, there was a sudden, dangerous silence. People stepped away from Mike, like a ripple of seawater pulling back off the shore. Harry hesitated. There was another way, between two of Mrs Green's wardrobes, a narrow gap. As he squeezed through, a black velvet-gloved hand grabbed him.

'They're doing us today.' Mrs Green's mother in her threadbare long coat smelled of mothballs. The two huge black feathers in her hat arched over him. 'You tell that soldier. If they forget, like yesterday, who's going to move all this inside again?'

Harry struggled free. 'They won't forget,' he said, and made a dash past the rest of the crowd.

Mike was waiting for him. Ahead, a black cart horse in brass regalia and a polished cart stood outside old Mr Thorn's cottage.

Chapter Eleven

A thin spiky man, all poky elbows and bony fingers, wearing a stiff black suit which was far too big for him, knelt on the floor beside the old armchair. Mud from his black shoes fell in nasty sticky little clods on the precious Victorian rug. Miss Markham got down on her knees too. Between them Abraham Thorn lay stretched out on the floor, his face grey and still.

'What's the matter with him?' Harry whispered to Mike.

Miss Markham smoothed back a wisp of the old man's hair. 'Just the fright of leaving home!'

In place of the wet and whiskery smile, old Mr Thorn's lips were dry and shrunken round his misfit teeth, but the wrinkles on his forehead were miraculously gone as if someone had ironed them out. He looked very cold and shiny. Frozen, as if he might be lying outside in deep snow without a coat. His favourite old black suit, he was wearing that. He'd shown it to Harry once. 'Souvenir of village celebrations for our dear Queen Victoria's Jubilee. I'd be pleased to die in it when time comes.'

Die. Harry felt Mike's steadying hand on his shoulder, but inside him his stomach churned. His feet seemed stuck to the floor. His ears were full of the ticking of the cracked clock on the wall... tick, tick, tick.

The spiky man looked up at Mike. A lock of thin hair fell over his long nose. 'Can you help us lift 'im up to put 'im in the box? Dead weight, he's a heavy old begger.'

Tick, tick, tick.

Frayed at the edges and shiny with old age, the jubilee jacket flapped forlornly over the undertaker's pokey arm. Mike took the head and the old crunched shoulders. Miss Markham took a firm grip of the trousers. They all grunted with the effort as they lifted. One of the feet fell back to the ground with a dull thud. The undertaker summoned Harry. 'You too, lad.'

Harry backed away, hearing in his head the quivering old voice, 'Not me! I'm not going!' Was it the bang, bang, bang of the walking stick, or that ticking clock, or his own heart thumping inside him?

'Come on, lad!' urged the undertaker, but Miss Markham was already rescuing the leg. Old Mr Thorn hovered in mid air, before they swung him over to the coffin, and lowered. The undertaker began to wedge him in.

Harry ran.

'Wait,' Mike called.

But Harry didn't. The freezing air outside surprised him into shallow sobbing breaths. He wanted to cry because the old man was Daddy's friend. His friend. But crying would be stupid, babyish. He wasn't going back inside though. He wanted to run to the beach, but somehow he couldn't do that either. He pressed his back hard against the garden wall. After a minute he hauled himself upwards and sat kicking at the wall with his heel. Ages passed before the undertaker and Mike carried the closed coffin out and heaved it onto the cart.

Miss Markham came out with a brown paper bag. 'Got your name on it.' Harry edged along the wall with it before her picky fingers could brush sand or something off his jacket.

Inside the bag was the red penknife that had sliced off juicy sticks of rhubarb, and hacked through thick stems of cabbage. With it the old man pricked off Brussels sprouts, and cut curly leaves of green kale. In the last couple of months he'd passed the knife over to Harry more often as the weather got colder and he moved more slowly, and his fingers were stiffer.

The red casing was smooth and familiar – and precious because Daddy had always used it too. Now Harry wished he'd come here this morning, or stayed yesterday. Why hadn't he made the old man hot tea, insisted on helping, or worked alone? Helped him pack up? He tugged fiercely at the shiny blade. It grunted out and glinted in the winter sunlight.

'Why don't you cut some flowers or something for old Mr Thorn, Harry?' Miss Markham suggested.

Near the wall was the one last rose, its pink petals cupped close in a perfect circle. A frail sweet scent came from it as he cut it. He passed it to Miss Markham and closed the knife. It gave the satisfying snap he knew so well. Miss Markham looked down at the rose for a moment, and dabbed her eye with her handkerchief.

Rhythmic puffs of breath misted out from the black nostrils of the old horse. As the undertaker steadied her, for some stupid reason Harry thought of Dad's train leaving – the steam, and like the train ones, these wheels, shifting, waiting to turn.

His anger burst out. 'It's all your fault,' he shouted at Mike. 'Why are you making us leave?'

The undertaker shook the reins. The horse

brasses and regalia jingled and the polished cart lurched forward. The wheels grated off over the ground and the horse's hooves clop-clopped away.

Miss Markham patted Mike's arm. 'We're all very grateful you boys are over here. You do know, don't you?' she said.

'Sure.'

Harry shaded his eyes and watched the undertaker slow to avoid the stacked furniture. The crowd parted. The WVS women there, distributing cups of tea, paused as the coffin passed them. The local boys, loading trucks and carts, lifted their caps. Even the GIs looked up.

The cart cleared the village and travelled out along the beach road. At the other end of the Sands it turned inland towards Slapton church.

Chapter Twelve

Harry burst in the front door. 'Come to the church!'

He stared round, surprised at the chaos. There were things all over the floor. Peppy was curled up in the corner of the sofa stroking a wooden spoon with her soft seagull feather, so far away in a dream of her own she didn't even look up. His Mum was crouching by the kitchen sink, frantically pulling more things out from the cupboard underneath.

'So you're back!' she said accusingly, without turning round. 'Are you deliberately staying out with those GIs so you don't have to help me pack?'

'He's dead, Mum.'

'What?' She leapt to her feet and stared at him, white faced.

'He's dead and Miss Markham was crying!'

'What?' she whispered. 'Who's dead?' Her hand reached out for the knitted shawl hanging over the chair, the one Daddy had wrapped round her shoulders in the dark, the night before he left.

'Where is Daddy really, Mum?'

The shawl snagged on a splinter on the chair's edge. 'He's in Italy,' she said, trying to release it. 'You know that, Harry. Away fighting.' Her fingers seemed bewildered by the entangled wool threads, the different colours.

'Where in Italy?'

'Missing.' There was a catch in her voice. Another thread of wool caught on the chair. 'You know that.' She tugged. That thread, then another, and another, all stretched to breaking point. Harry heard a squeak from the corner. Peppy was up and pressed against sofa, her little eyes wide. In a second he'd go over and hug her, but right now he needed answers. 'What if Daddy comes home, we've gone and he can't find us?'

His mother ripped the shawl to her and hugged it tight. The knitting began unravelling, rick-racking away from the broken threads. 'Lewis tells me you're in trouble now for beating up young Frank Prouse. Harry!'

'He's dead and gone to Slapton church.'

'Who? Who is dead?'

'Old Mr Thorn, Mum. You coming?'

Her fingers dug deep into the wool. 'What do I want with death?' she cried, holding up the torn shawl to inspect the damage. More strands sprang away through the stitching.

He stared at her through the huge gaping hole. What was the matter with her?

She folded the shawl quickly and put it down on the table among the confusion of kitchen things. 'You haven't packed,' she said, trying to sound calm. 'Go and pack.'

'Mrs Gale said her husband was safe now. Did she mean he was dead?'

Her face screwed into distress. 'Grow up, Harry. This is war!'

'You don't care about me, what I feel!'

'I care about you packing up!' she cried. 'I care what will happen to us!'

He turned defiantly and darted back out into lane. He could hear her shouting after him. 'Harry! Harry! Come back here!'

But he was off and running far too fast.

There were heavy wooden crates stacked on the path and parts of the precious carved rood screens leaning against the porch wall. The organ inside sounded muffled and weird.

Coloured light from the stained glass windows fell across the simple coffin lying by the altar steps. The church was full of people. Harry crept down the side aisle and slid into a pew. Now he could see why Amy Wardle's playing sounded strange. There were sandbags placed round the base of the organ pipes, dulling them, muffling the notes. As Amy finished the last chords of the hymn, a man in dark flowing robes swept in through a side door. He glanced in surprise at all the people and climbed up into the partly dismantled pulpit. An old carpenter quietly unscrewing the font in the side chapel put his screwdriver in the pocket of his leather apron and sat down too. Harry felt for the penknife in his pocket and brought it out onto his lap.

In a sudden silence several people coughed. He heard someone whisper: 'Who'd have thought the old beggar would have the Bishop of Exeter praying over him!' and someone else's angry, 'Ssh!'

The Bishop cleared his throat. 'Today,' he began, 'we are gathered here in Slapton church to say goodbye to...' he paused...

'Abraham Thorn,' prompted Amy.

'Our brother, Abraham. Well, I must be brief. There are church valuables to be packed. We are all very busy. I am, and so are you. There is a great deal still to be done before...' His words hung on the air as he cast a solemn eye across the expectant congregation. He cleared his throat again. 'People have told me old Mr Thorn, as you all called him, never ventured more than eight miles from his home in Torcross. That's about as far as the other end of Slapton Sands. A walk to the end of the beach and back. Not far for a whole life.'

Harry wished he'd chosen a different pew. If Miss Markham looked this way, he was in her direct line of sight. Beside her Farmer Mitchelmay stared fixedly at the coffin. Mary Hayton, and several other village people sat nearby. He wondered when they all finally left, where they were all going.

The Bishop continued. 'Right now so many you are leaving your homes and stepping bravely into an unknown future.'

On the coffin lay the rose he'd picked from old Mr Thorn's garden, that last rose, its petals already limp and fading from their soft blush of pink.

'Families like yours have been here for generations. Many of you, like old Mr Thorn, were born here and you've lived here all your days. In his long life Abraham Thorn never packed up his few possessions or travelled to another town or a new county as you are preparing to do. But as we think about the life of

Abraham today, here in this church, we know he has travelled further now than any one of us. He has made the longest journey any of us ever makes, the final one. We pray today that he has arrived in his father's house… to a place of safety and everlasting peace.'

'Amen,' said Amy Wardle, from her seat at the organ.

A place of safety? Mr Gale's place of safety?

The Bishop took a moment to turn a page in his notes. 'We live in a time of uncertainty. We feel afraid for ourselves, for our children, for our loved ones. We feel afraid for all the men fighting now so that we might be safe. And grief for the men who will never come home. We miss them all, the sons, the husbands, and the fathers who are so far away.'

Harry swallowed and focused very hard on the coffin.

'In his Christmas broadcast four years ago the King quoted verses by Minnie Louise Haskins. Perhaps her faith will help us all again today as we pack up and prepare to travel along the long hard road ahead.

'"I said to the man who stood at the gate of the year, Give me a light that I might tread safely into the* *unknown. And he replied, Go out into the darkness and put your hand into the hand of God. That shall be to you better than light and safer than a known way!"'*

For a moment there was silence. Then the Bishop quietly closed his book. 'Let all of us take the hand of God today,' he said, 'and sing together. Psalm number twenty-three.'

Amy Wardle struck up the familiar notes on the organ. People shuffled and stumbled to their feet.

It was comforting to sing, and this psalm was Daddy's favourite. Harry knew it well and he began confidently enough… *The Lord's my shepherd, I shall not want…* But there were things he did want. Like staying here and Daddy coming back, and Mum being like she used to be. And Peppy not feeling frightened. And why leave these green pastures? What about all those animals at the auction? And the still waters? This sea wasn't going to be his anymore. And old Mr Thorn was gone.

Amy Wardle pressed hard on the pedals. The music reverberated through the church with the dangerous penultimate verse: *And though I walk through death's dark vale…*

Harry's voice faltered inside him, caught and wouldn't come out of his throat. An angry tear ran down his cheek. He wiped it away roughly. Now Miss Markham was looking along the row, watching him, worrying about him. He pulled back out of her sight, but he heard her voice rising and leading, strong and clear. The congregation's singing swelled and lifted. *And in God's house forever more, my dwelling place shall be...*

But when Daddy came home, how would he find out where that house would be?

Chapter Thirteen

'Ever been to a wake, Harry?' asked Mike, passing him a glass of cola. 'I guess that's what this is.'

Harry had found him waiting outside the church, and they'd walked silently together to the Queen's Arms Public House. Everyone else was there, Mary Hayton, Amy, and her father-in-law, old Mr Wardle, Farmer Mitchelmay and two other farmers, Reg Thompson, Miss Markham, and even surprisingly, Jed. What about the fields?

Harry could feel Mike looking at him.

'Sorry about the old man.'

He glanced away, the cloying sweetness of the cola sinking into his tongue.

'Your mum won't mind you being here?'

Harry shook his head. Right now he didn't care if she did. He took another sip of cola, smelled the stale mix of cigarette smoke and ale, and listened to the farmers muttering over in the snug. 'They straightened that lane on account them GIs drive too fast. Other lanes too. And widened 'em.'

'It's the bulldozing I hate,' said the other.

'Those ancient hedges shaped my land since the Doomsday book. It's vandalism.'

'Reckon the invasion must be soon.'

'Ssh! There's Yanks here.'

Mike might have heard that but he just took a sip of his beer. 'Warm,' he said, wrinkling his nose.

Another GI sat wistfully playing Blues on the piano in the far corner.

'Who's he?' asked Harry.

'One of our guys,' said Mike. 'Any piano, anywhere, he's up for it.'

'Will we be invaded?' Harry asked. 'Is that why you're here?'

But at that moment there was a loud burst of laughter. 'Was! So I was!' Mary Hayton was blushing as red as her hair. 'The spiders was worst! I felt 'em crawling on me for weeks!'

'Saved your life, that thatch, spiders 'n all,' said Mary's father-in-law.

The landlady Annie came along behind the bar to wash a glass. She nodded to Mike. 'Stray bomb she's talking about,' she explained. 'Left over from that night's air raid on Plymouth. The Haytons had a shop and two cottages on the sea front.'

The dull thud of explosion shuddered through

Harry's head again, the sound of wood splintering and glass shattering in cold clear night air. And in the fall out, his father's voice: 'No-one's safe. Not even here…'

'Night the last of our men decided to go,' Annie said.

Harry took a nervous gulp of cola.

'You okay?' asked Mike.

'Yes.'

'Whole lot collapsed,' Mary went on dramatically.

Annie moved back along the bar again to join the amusement. 'The thatch lifted and dropped in one piece, Mary, didn't it? Like a huge tea-cosy.'

'Smothered us in dust and old hay. Spiders…'

'Whole family walked away luckily.' Amy laughed. 'Not a scratch.'

'I was scratched!' protested Mary. 'And sneezing for weeks, I was!'

Annie was pointing back along the bar. Harry ducked down, but Miss Markham was already making her way over.

'We'll give 'em back more than dust and spiders if they come here!' said Reg, raising his glass high.

'But day after tomorrow we won't be here,' said one of the farmers. 'Will we?'

The pianist had just finished playing.

'Can't you play anything British?' called Jed, swaying and waving his beer glass at him dramatically. He'd seen Mike too. 'You GIs want to be careful. Tis said this sea is stained with blood in winter storms.'

'Take no notice of him,' said Miss Markham, arriving in time to pat Mike's arm. 'It's red sandstone. The cliffs, they crumble in rough seas.'

'It is real red, the soil round here,' Mike agreed. 'Strange liver colour.'

'It sticks to you,' said Harry quietly.

'Good British soil! And it's ours!'

Who called that? One of the farmers?

'And where are we meant to go?'

'Best soil in the country, this.' Reg lifted his empty glass. 'Better'n Dartmouth.'

'Don't want to go to Dartmouth,' said Jed. 'Or Plymouth. Them's naval. Dangerous. Nobody wants to move there.'

'Forced off our own land.' The farmers again.

'Never'd go near London,' said Amy.

'Or Coventry,' agreed Mary. 'Them industrial places.'

'Tis our home, this.'

'We've been here all our lives,' said Miss Markham quietly. 'No one wants to go anywhere really.'

Jed banged his empty beer mug down on the bar and glared at Mike. 'So what's the GI here for?'

Sudden silence. Mike put down his beer.

'He's been helping people. I've seen him.' The words rushed out of Harry's mouth so fast and loud it surprised him. And he heard his voice get even louder. 'Mrs Gale. He gave her some money to take her husband on the train.'

'Ha!'

They were all staring at him now, Amy, Miss Markham, everyone.

'He's just doing his job. He helped you carry your sideboard you don't know what you'll do with, Kathleen.' He took another breath. 'And he didn't chase old Mr Wardle, Amy.'

'And what are you doing here, boy?' demanded Jed. 'Spying for your mother's Warden?'

Harry glared at Jed. He felt as if he might be sick.

'You've been drinking too much too long, Jed Trow,' said Miss Markham.

'Old Abraham would never have shouted at 'em except for that kid,' Jed countered.

'He shouted pretty loud at the public meeting

as I recall,' said Amy.

Mike took Harry's empty glass from him and put it ready on the bar. 'Harry's here because he was the old guy's best friend,' he said. There was silence.

Miss Markham nodded. 'So he was.'

'Him, and his father too,' said Reg.

'Spitting image,' said Jed.

Harry felt his throat tighten as they all looked hard at him, into him, at his father in him.

'Celia's boy,' said Amy, as if to remind them.

He heard someone whisper, 'Any news of John?' and Amy looked away.

'All our boys are gone,' said Mary's father-in-law. 'All our farming men.'

'Can I buy you all a drink?' asked Mike. 'For old Mr Thorn?'

Silence again.

Mike put his hand on Harry's shoulder. 'For friendship?'

Jed looked at Harry. 'Go on then, for old Abraham.'

'Better drink it than pack it up,' said Annie.

'Remember the dog that blew up the mine that blew up the Royal Sands Hotel?' said Mary.

'And closed it for the duration,' said Annie triumphantly. 'So now there's just us here at the

Queen's Arms! And the GI's paying. Who wants what?'

At the piano the other GI began to play again and sing: 'So long Mom, we won't be gone for long…' Three more GIs lurched in the door. They heard the song and gathered round the piano, cheerfully joining in. '…so send in the marines and get it done!'

'They all sound so confident,' Amy said. 'Maybe the war won't last much longer now they're here.'

'We're doing this for you, you know, kid. So you can be free,' Mike said, before he left him. Harry wondered quite what that meant. Doing what? Moving everyone?

He walked back alone, though Mike had offered to come. Following the thin beam of light from Daddy's old pocket torch towards home was comforting.

By the empty seafront houses he paused, sniffed the salt on the air and gazed back along the coast. The moon broke cover and shone majestically over the bay. The choppy indigo sea was spattered with silver light. Far out on the horizon was the dark threat of a war ship.

Why did the Americans want his beach? If they

really wanted to help, couldn't they just go and fight the enemy?

Chapter Fourteen

Dawn, and his mum was up making more chaos out of packing. All the same Harry couldn't think what was different when he came back inside from the lav. He stamped the frost off his shoes and looked round. The boxes were all tied up now and ready. A battered suitcase lay open on the table, nearly full of clothes. Next to it were two pairs of sheets. Pillow slips. Down on the floor was a cloth sack with kitchen utensils sticking out of it.

He shivered and took the poker and scratched around in the layer of potato peelings in the grate. He added a couple of new sticks of wood. What was left of last night's fire smouldering underneath flamed up afresh. He held the kettle under the creaky old tank tap. The water trickled, struggling through frigid pipe.

'I don't want you helping those GIs, Harry. We're all being forced out of our homes, our jobs. I don't know what we're meant to do.' His mum was stacking ironed sheets inside the cupboard under the stairs. At her feet were pots and pans, and Dad's good jacket, folded, and his fishing gear.

'Aren't we taking those?'

'Six months they said. I want to have something here to come back to.'

'Kathleen's taking her mother's sideboard.'

'Well, isn't she the lucky one?' She emerged with a cobweb in her hair and two folded sheets over her arm. 'We'll take these. There's no knowing what kind of arrangements there'll be.'

Harry listened suddenly into the silence. 'Where's Peppy?'

His mother nodded over to the sofa. He saw her frown, glance around. 'Peppy?'

In his room his best shells were scattered on his bed.

Mum leapt up the loft stairs and then back down them. 'Where is she?' There was panic in her voice. She glanced at the front door, and then turned on him. 'Is your window open?'

They were out in the street in a second.

'Peppy? Peppy?'

One way, further up, the steep cliff edge and sharp rocks below. The other...

'Go that way, Harry,' she screamed, pointing down at people, trucks, bicycles, streaming away along the coast road. She darted away up the hill herself. 'Run!'

He ran.

'I'll do the Ley lane,' she shrieked back.

Dust clouded up from trucks, horses and carts, bikes, wheelbarrows, old prams. People were off before the next day's final deadline.

Harry ran along, searching every group, asking. 'My little sister? You know her. Fair hair? Two years old. Have you seen her?' Nobody had.

He darted back to the corner shouting her name. He dodged the old steam tractor puffing, ready to tow out the huge threshing machine. Emerging from the thick cloud of steam and wheat dust behind it crawled a smart black motorcar. The uniformed driver glared at Harry leaning anxiously in the back window. 'Hands orff! We might be helping you lot, but show some respect for the motor.' The sheep farming family crammed inside stared at Harry. 'My little sister? Have you seen her?' They shook their heads. 'Your dad back?' they asked.

He peeled away without answering, scared now. A dreadful picture of Peppy running out into the busy road combined in his head with the sight of an old farm truck lurching uncontrollably down the hill. Two moth-eaten mattresses, a rusty bed rail, table, chairs, and other scruffy belongings were roped on, and top of the pile was Lillie, jolting along, clinging on. Jed waved from the rattling cab.

Harry waved both arms at him.

'Peppy? Jed,' he shouted, 'have you seen her?'

'Keep safe, lad,' was all Jed called back.

'Where's Tim?' But Jed didn't hear that either.

Harry wheeled round and ran out onto the coast road, sprinting ahead of the black motorcar, past the bicycles, horses and carts, wheelbarrows, prams. Passing everything now because they were slowing up and halting. Way out in front, nothing was moving. Everyone, everything, was waiting.

Tim was there. 'Our Peppy,' Harry gasped. 'She's disappeared.'

They hunted together now. Running back all the way to the village, shouting Peppy's name. Scanning the crowd. Asking. Calling.

'The beach?'

'Come on!' Breathless, they nipped through the Cut.

Suddenly Harry saw her. Silhouetted dark against sparkling. Playing with slate stones on the water's edge. He was first there, scooping her up. She laughed out loud as he danced around, crowing her name with delight, hugging her tight. She held up a piece of shiny grey slate.

His mum was running down the shingle now. She snatched Peppy, clutched her close, tears streaming down her face. She glanced at the long procession on the main road and angrily back at Harry. Then she turned and carried Peppy back up the beach. Over her shoulder, Peppy waved back at him. And somehow, he didn't know why, he felt angry and empty and disappointed. He kicked at the shiny wet pebbles, at pieces of beautiful ridged grey slate by the water's edge.

'But you found Peppy,' said Tim. 'Didn't your mum see that?'

Chapter Fifteen

All eyes turned inland to the north-east approach, as Harry and Tim walked back along the sea front. 'Where are you going?' Harry asked, still edgy. 'Do you know?'

'They're coming,' said Tim. 'Listen!'

A distant thrum. At first Harry could only make out a column of grey crawling down the hill road. Chugging, wheezing, rumbling. Then trucks advanced along the coast road, their covering canvasses billowing out, and their windscreens flashing sunlight like Morse code. Behind them, the tighter, smaller outline of jeeps. Behind that, the first glimpses of sombre lumbering tanks.

Heavy wheels and revving engines rumbled louder, closer. A fume of fuel drifted in on the air. Children on the dunes started to cry. People on the road in front of Harry stepped back, holding on tight to their belongings. GI outriders in two fast jeeps rattled in to clear the road ahead.

Lewis was with them, leaping out and shouting the US Army has right of way. Forcing local vehicles aside. Thumping car windscreens. Shoving people, flexing and clenching his muscular arms, a policeman's truncheon in hand and his key chain rattling at his waist, insisting anyone, anything, pull right off the road. Anything on wheels, or on foot. On his order, bikes, carts and prams lurched into rabbit holes and sand ditches. He took no argument, used force where it wasn't needed. 'That's how it all starts,' someone muttered. 'Some bully takes charge.'

Harry felt his fists clenching as he watched startled families retreat away from Lewis and up onto the slopes of the dunes, clutching their frightened children.

The convoy passed, and passed, and passed. American trucks roared by, GIs looking out expectantly. British soldiers too. Equipment lorries, jeeps, endless armoured cars.

'All this. And all on our side,' Tim shouted to him above the din.

The haze of sour diesel fumes filled Harry's nostrils. The tanks rolled by, engines deafening him, crunching wheels and chains biting deep into the weak road surface. He imagined the huge guns on top of them firing, the flash, the explosive power bursting straight at him. But no shots were firing here. Just Lewis shouting government orders to leave. Everyone letting him push them around, and allowing these troops to take over their homes, their land, their beach.

Back waiting on the village corner was something bigger than the tanks, something older, more cumbersome. Harry nudged Tim. 'Look!'

The US column slowed up. Halted. Trucks began backing up, forcing the vehicles behind them to do the same. People on the dunes leaned out to see, broke ranks and moved forward. Then a breathless whoo-hoop and a distant blast of thick white steam.

Tim grinned at him. 'Hey!'

Down by the Ley turn, the huge threshing machine lumbered out, drawn by Farmer Mitchelmay in his steam tractor. Amusement rippled through the locals as bewildered US officers stood up in their jeeps to see what the hold-up was. They glowered as vehicles ahead of them were forced into retreat. They swore as they had to reverse their own vehicles and pull over and wait. They read and re-read their maps, tapped their feet, kicked their rubber tyres. Waited, as everyone here had waited for them. Harry and Tim climbed higher on the dunes to see better. And when finally the thresher broke through, its metal wheels squealing along the surface of the coast road, there was cheering. Everyone surged forward and waved and shouted as the thresher growled slowly past. Someone shouted God Save the King, and Farmer Mitchelmay tooted his tractor steam whistle and waved.

'It's just like the village fete,' laughed Tim. And they waved and cheered, and cheered some more.

But after the thresher passed and pulled away into the empty distance, and the last Americans moved off again shouting *Let's go*, and *Forward you men*, everyone who had been cheering went quiet. Prams and barrows were hauled out of the ditches and onto the road. Old truck doors slammed. Engines spluttered back to life. Old rusty cart wheels rolled again. Some of the people on foot began to cut up through the fields.

'Nobody wants to stay now,' Harry said.

Tim didn't answer. He was watching the grand black motorcar approaching, and Jed waving from the old truck right behind it.

'Where will you be?' Harry asked, as it drew closer.

'I found a fly in a currant bun last week,' Tim

said. Harry stared at him. 'Go on,' said Tim. 'Ask me!'

'Go on then. I'm asking.'

'Mrs Prouse said if I took it back, she'd exchange it for a currant.' He grinned. Jed's truck was level with them.

'So where? Where will you be?' The truck was rattling on, passing them now, gaining speed.

'See you,' Tim said, keeping his eyes fixed on Harry as he backed away along the road.

'Where, Tim?'

Tim turned and chased after the truck. He caught it up, grabbed at the bed rail and launched himself upwards. The roped-on furniture swayed dangerously. It looked as if the whole lot might collapse. Lillie clung on desperately. Tim hauled himself higher as the truck lurched on. Finally at the top of the pile and when the load's violent swaying subsided, he waved triumphantly.

Harry stood squinting along the coast road till his best friend was too far away to see.

Chapter Sixteen

Harry sat for a while in the hide listening to the sea. Tucked between stones was the old map of the Devon coast he and Dad had drawn. It was a bit screwed up and ragged round the edges but it was worth keeping. He put it in his pocket. He took care when he climbed out but there was no-one left now to see him. Down by the water's edge he collected some round white pebbles for Peppy. There were still a few families heading out on the coast road, but most people were already gone. The lagoon was still. The village behind it was deserted. Over on the hill the US accommodation camp was busy.

In the church cemetery he watched a man shovelling earth out of a hole, digging a new grave. Old Mr Thorn's coffin sat waiting beside it.

On the other side of the narrow lane a climbing rose bush hung over the Chantry garden wall and wound up into the footbridge. The grand old house was American military territory now, their headquarters. The gates were open and GIs were gathered round a big metal drum of boiling water, laughing and talking. Layers of wood smoke, and steam, and the enticing smell of fresh coffee thickened the cold morning air.

Further down the lane he looked up at the ruined tower, all that was left of an ancient monastery. Henry VIII had destroyed it. A few hundred years back, the king sent in his army and scared the local people away. Things here changed back then too.

He climbed over the ivy covered wall of the church yard. By the gate Mike and two other GIs were loading the last of the carefully packed church valuables into the Bishop's car.

'Young and old.'

The ivy rustled as Harry pressed back into its shadow.

The Bishop sat with pen and paper on a fallen grave, his flowing black robes hanging over a rash of gold lichen. He seemed to be talking to himself. 'People have lived in these houses and tilled these fields ever since there was a church. A community, here for years, several hundred years.' He held up the paper and read. 'This church, this churchyard where their loved ones lie at rest...' He glanced over at the gate as a GI disappeared through it with another box. Then he wrote on the paper, held it up, cleared his throat. '...these homes, these fields are as dear to those that have left them as the homes and fields which you, our allies, have left behind. They hope to return one day, as you hope to return to yours, to find them waiting to welcome them home.' He glanced at his watch, wrapped his scarf more firmly round his neck, and added a few more words to the page. 'All out?' he called over to the GIs. They nodded. He rose and looked up at the spire. 'They entrust them to your care and pray God's blessing rests upon us all.'

He pulled the old church door shut and Mike nailed the piece of paper to it. Then the Bishop strode out to his car and was driven off. The GIs disappeared behind the church. Harry peered at the Bishop's notice. It was addressed: TO OUR ALLIES FROM THE USA.

Mike was piling sandbags up the belfry wall towards the stained glass window. 'Off then, Harry?' he asked cheerfully.

'Tomorrow.'

'Where?'

Harry shrugged. Over in the graveyard he could see two GIs helping the farm worker lower old Abraham Thorn's coffin into the ground. 'Will you play killing games? When's the invasion?'

Mike balanced the sandbag he was holding against the belfry wall. 'Look, I might not see you again, Harry Beere.'

Harry pushed his hands deeper into the rubber bands and rubbish in his pockets. 'No one ever answers anything.'

Over in the grave yard the farm worker took up his shovel. A first shower of earth went back into the grave.

'Look kid, you don't want to worry about all this. That old guy was... old.'

'I'm not talking about him. It's my daddy. He's missing in Italy.'

'Missing?'

'That's what Mum says. What if he comes home and we're not here?'

Two rooks began to circle the tall church spire.

'He'll find you.'

'What happens to dead soldiers? Are they buried?'

Mike took the sandbag's full weight back and heaved it up and onto the heap. 'Yes.'

'Where?'

Mike dusted sand off his sleeve and frowned. 'Got to be where they die right now. Where they fall.' He glanced over at the graveyard himself. 'Some corner of a foreign field.' After a moment he reached into his pocket. 'I sure am going miss you, Harry Beere.'

Harry shook his head at the offered gum. 'What if no one buries them? What if no one even knows?'

Mike looked at him carefully. 'Time takes care of it, I guess.'

'What? Bones and stuff?'

'Uh, huh.' Mike opened a gum for himself, peeling the wrapping back very slowly.

'And some soldiers never come home?'

'That's right.' Mike looked up at the black rooks circling one more time. Then they dipped and flapped out across the chill blue sky to the high hill pastures. 'But I guess they get remembered,' he said. 'If they don't come home, the people who love them remember them.'

'Is that all?'

Mike considered it. 'Maybe that's all any of us get, Harry,' he said. 'Maybe being remembered is the best sort of love.'

In the dim lamp light Harry sat on his bed with an empty cardboard box, surrounded by all his belongings, looking at his dad's photo, worrying. What could Peppy remember? She wasn't even born when Daddy went.

'Lewis will be here first thing in the morning,' his mother called from the kitchen.

'Who's Lewis?'

She stuck her head round the door. 'You know very well who Mr Cramer is.'

'But who is he really, Mum?' He gazed at her.

'Harry, you know all this.'

She didn't seem to want to understand. 'Where are we going?' he asked instead.

'Totnes.'

'What's it like? How will Daddy know?'

'Please, Harry. Tomorrow's the deadline.'

'Do you remember Daddy?'

'Of course!' She looked at him as if she might suddenly cry. 'You need to get packing,' she said.

'Okay,' he said, feeling guilty, giving in.

She gave him a watery smile and went back to see if Peppy was asleep and do whatever it was she was doing in the kitchen. Why was she fussing so much about him packing? It wouldn't take any time to put his things into the box. He wrapped the shells and his other beach mementoes inside his spare vest and his two pairs of threadbare socks. There were his goggles Tim had found and given him, and a couple of half used exercise books from school he probably should take. He put in his two decent pencils. He could leave his old ink pen behind. No point in it leaking on everything. The penknife could go in his pocket and he'd wear his gloves and scarf. The old bits of driftwood didn't need much protection, but the precious photo of Daddy did. He pulled stuff out and re-packed, wrapping it carefully in his old sweater. There was nothing else except the clothes he was wearing and would put on again in the morning. Packing was easy. It was the leaving he didn't want to do.

He could hear her moving round the kitchen, still putting things into boxes.

'Night,' he called.

He said it louder. Still no answer.

Reaching down the side of the box he found one of the pencils. On the wall beside his bed he wrote as thick and dark as he could: *DEAR DADDY, T O T N I S*. Then underneath that he wrote smaller, *HB* and *Peppy B*.

He put out the light, opened the blackout curtain and climbed into bed, and for the last time he lay listening to the sound of the sea. Just once he thought he heard sobbing, but then the wind rose suddenly and the tide began to jiggle urgently up the shingle, drowning out the night. He drifted into deep sleep, dreaming of running along the beach, chasing something. Calling...

Chapter Seventeen

His box sat behind the front door. In the centre of the room were other boxes and belongings ready to go. Somewhere under the dustsheets Peppy was singing away to herself.

'Aren't we taking anything, Mum? Mrs Green took all her furniture.'

'We're coming back, Harry! We'll make do with whatever is at the lodging house.' She was checking and re-checking, running round finding small last minute items to stuff into one last box. 'Why don't I have another suitcase?' she wailed, surveying the pile of boxes. 'Why don't I have anything respectable?'

In his room his window was wide open to the salt air. Old sheets were draped over his bed and chest of drawers. The writing was on the wall.

A car was coming up the lane. He saw his mum pull on her coat and run her hands through her hair to tidy it. The car door slammed and Lewis came straight in. He had nylon stockings for her. 'To cheer you up,' he said.

She looked at them, thrilled. 'Lewis!'

'It's going to rain. Get the boy moving these

boxes.'

'Harry?'

Out in Start Bay rain was streaking in along the horizon. Harry ran from one person to another asking. There were just a handful, quietly moving around. Like people on newsreels, they seemed to flicker in the diminishing light, like ghosts. When the sun came out later they would all be gone. Right now they worked silently and quickly, too busy to be angry or afraid anymore. There was a deadline of one more hour. More US army vehicles were lined up all along the coast road waiting.

Mary Hayton was loading her father's battered old car.

'Who's staying behind?' Harry asked her.

'No one, Harry,' she said, manoeuvring round him with a pile of bedding.

'How will anyone know where everyone's gone? Say someone comes?'

She stuffed the bedding onto the back seat between her distracted old dog and two baskets of squawking chickens. 'Shh! Shh!' She turned back to him. 'What? You mean an invasion?' She didn't seem scared to say it. He shook his head. 'Who?' she demanded. 'Who will come?'

He looked away, agitated, searching for someone else to ask. There wasn't anyone else. He persevered. 'My Dad. Will it be listed where we've gone?'

'There were forms, Harry,' Mary said. 'Ask Miss Markham.'

The shop doorbell tinkled as he stepped in from the spotting rain. The post office was all bare shelves and empty slots now. In the back stockroom he could see a ladder, and on the top rung, stout lace up shoes and thick ankles. The rest of her was somewhere up above.

'Miss Markham?'

'Wait on, I'm just getting these last things down.' He fidgeted, idly running his finger along the counter. The surface was as clean as a whistle. He wondered if his mother was leaving their cottage so tidy.

The ankles moved down two rungs of the ladder. 'Won't be a moment.'

The bell jangled, the door flew open. A hand grabbed his shoulder. 'Your mother's waiting. Think we've got all day?'

'There's forms,' Harry protested, trying to twist free from the iron grip. 'My dad needs to know where we've gone.'

Lewis pushed him to the door. 'Your mother will have taken care of that.'

Harry swung back. 'Miss Markham?'

The feet came down three more steps. 'Just coming.'

'Don't you listen, boy?' said Lewis, dragging him by the collar. 'Come on! Or you and your mother can find other transport.'

The car was packed, and Peppy settled in too.

'Where were you?' his mum cried. 'Lewis had to do it all. Check the kitchen window quick, and the back door.'

They were securely locked. Harry gaped out at the water dripping down from that broken gutter his dad never got round to mending.

Mum was beside him now, checking the door and window herself. The rain, first spitting at the glass, fell faster, running down the window in greasy rivulets. 'I should have cleaned it,' she wailed.

Lewis called. 'Go on, Harry, go on,' she said, pushing him ahead, and plumping up the cushion on the worn old sofa and pulling the dustsheet back over it. 'Go on!'

'Get in, boy,' growled Lewis.

Peppy reached out across the boxes on the

back seat as Harry climbed into the car. He gave her fingers a reassuring squeeze. He turned back to watch his mum on the doorstep closing the front door, turning the key in the lock.

'I never said goodbye to Amy,' she said tearfully, as she climbed into the car.

Out on the coast road they passed bedraggled stragglers pushing or carrying their belongings, heading for the hills driven by shafts of rain. Lines of military vehicles thundered past the other way. Lewis boasted he had borrowed this smart army car specially. 'Extra allowance of petrol just for you, love,' he bragged.

'Everyone leaving is allowed that,' Harry muttered. Behind them, the bay was misting over with rain.

His mum wasn't looking back. She was searching her handbag. Harry could almost feel her panic. 'I can't find it!'

'What, Mum?'

'What?' asked Lewis, negotiating his way past a family struggling on the road with an unwieldy cart.

Harry leaned forward anxiously. 'What?'

'I can't think,' said Celia. 'Something.' She turned round to him. 'What's in the back?'

'Where are my things?' he demanded

suddenly. 'Where's my box?'

Celia caught her breath, horrified.

'You forgot my box?'

Lewis swerved the steering wheel impatiently, forcing some walkers to leap off the road in fright. 'What now?'

'Mum!'

'His clothes and things,' she said.

'He can wear what he's in.'

'We have to go back, Mum!'

'Behave yourself, boy!'

'But we have to!'

'Sssh, Harry. We can't,' whispered Celia.

'But there's Daddy's photo!'

'Whatever you've left behind is not important now,' growled Lewis, taking a hand off the steering wheel to wave Celia back to facing front.

Harry grabbed at Lewis's shoulder. 'It is important!'

Lewis veered angrily off the road and screeched to a halt. 'Look, boy!'

Celia sounded scared. 'Some things have to be sacrificed, Harry! Do you think I could bring everything I wanted?'

Was she siding with Lewis? 'You left it behind on purpose,' Harry shouted. Peppy began to cry.

'Behave yourself, Harry! Behave yourself in

front of Mr Cramer!'

'No!'

'Silence,' roared Lewis, starting the engine
again. Celia shrank down in her seat. Harry
slumped back in disbelief. Peppy stared across to
him, sobbing. He reached out to comfort her.

'Here! Give her to me.' Celia leaned round and
hauled Peppy over into the front.

Harry sat in angry silence watching the rain
hissing against the foggy windows. In the front
Peppy was quiet now, frightened into silence by
the nearness of Lewis, or perhaps just lulled by
the motion of the car. Lewis reached into his top
pocket and produced a lipstick. Harry watched
his mum remove the cover. He could see she was
thrilled as she slowly pushed up the blood red
stick. 'Oh!' She held it up and away from Peppy's
enquiring little fingers. Lewis shot her a really
charming smile. 'It'll look just fine on those pretty
lips,' he said.

Harry stared tearfully out the back window.
The rain had cleared the bay and was chasing
them up the hill. Celia glanced round
sympathetically. 'The beach will still be there
when we come back.'

On the road ahead more people struggled with
carts and possessions. Three thousand people

were on the move – he'd heard that in the Queen's Arms – three thousand people leaving their homes behind, going who knew where, and not knowing why.

Chapter Eighteen

In the dark hall they waited, dripping wet, surrounded by their belongings. Celia clutched one of the bags, while Peppy pressed in heavily against Harry's shoulder, clingy and anxious. Lewis lurked behind them.

Their new landlady had deep lines etched round her prim mouth, and a sharp pointed nose like a hawk's beak. Her shawl hung in folds round her shoulders like black wings. She glanced down angrily at the puddle of water they were causing and stretched out her hand.

Lewis handed over a folded ten shilling note. Celia shot him a grateful smile. 'It's so kind of you to have us, Mrs Latcham,' she said.

Mrs Latcham sniffed and secreted the money somewhere into her clothing. 'The war, Mrs Beere, requires us all to do our duty.' Harry felt her critical eye on him. Peppy buried her face deep into his neck and clung on tighter.

'Bring something, Harry,' instructed Celia, taking Peppy from him. He picked up one of the boxes and they all followed Mrs Latcham upstairs.

The accommodation consisted of two small rooms. His mother's room, the larger one, overlooked the street. It had two beds, a basin, a cracked wall mirror, a gas ring for boiling water, and a battered old wireless. There were coin meters for gas and electric. 'You'll want pennies for those,' said Mrs Latcham. 'It's sixpence if you want me to lend you the bath tap.' There was a musty smell about her that made Harry wonder if she ever used the bath herself.

His room, no more than a box room, had a connecting door from the first room, and another door onto the landing. There was just space for a narrow bed and a chest of drawers. In one corner the dark stained wallpaper peeled away from the wall, and in another corner were black mildew spots. Through his small window Mrs Latcham pointed a bony finger down into a narrow back yard. 'Outside lav,' she said.

'Fine. It's fine,' said Celia. 'Isn't it, Harry?' She nudged him to be polite, but it wasn't fine. Why did he have to say it was?

'It's to be kept properly,' said Mrs Latcham.

'Of course,' said Celia. 'Thank you.' With that Mrs Latcham nodded and left them. The first thing Lewis did was try the door between the two rooms to make sure it would close.

'Go down for the rest of the things, Harry,' said Celia, sitting Peppy on her new lumpy bed.

Harry glanced angrily at Lewis. There was tons of stuff to bring upstairs. Why did he have to do it all? Out on the landing he waited and listened.

'It's awful,' hissed Celia.

'Best I could get,' Lewis said, 'since you wanted to keep the boy.'

Harry drew back shocked.

'How long's the kid taking? It's a simple task.'

Harry crept downstairs. A door down there was open. The old hawk, he decided that would be a good name for her – must be watching him. He loaded himself up with the most he could carry and struggled back upstairs.

'I'll take you out then. Eight o'clock,' he heard Lewis saying. 'Meet me outside.'

Celia's voice was muffled. 'But Lewis, it's their first night.'

'Come on, love! They're okay here. You want me to help you, don't you?'

Harry pushed against the door and squeezed through with his load. Lewis snatched one of the boxes from him and put it on the bed, as if he'd carried it all the way. And she thanked him!

At the door he turned. 'Later,' he said firmly.

All the boxes were up. One had an H on the side. 'It was for Christmas,' she said, handing it to him, 'but you need it now.'

He fumbled opening it, and let Peppy help him so it took longer. Inside was a knitted jumper, one of Miss Markham's best efforts, and a pair of short trousers. Apart from what he was standing up in, this was all he had now.

'Thanks,' he said gruffly. When she took Peppy back into her room looking disappointed, he wished he'd said thank you better. He could say something nice, that the navy jumper was a good colour or something, but he didn't want to. It was horrid here. Through the middle doorway he could see her unpacking, making the bed with their own sheets, talking to Peppy. That distance thing lay between them again, exaggerated by the sound of heavy rain on the roof and water leaking from some horrible broken gutter outside his window.

Five o'clock, and the daylight was already gone. He heard a hiss up the stairs. 'Harry?' He went out on the landing. Mum beckoned up to him and disappeared back into the kitchen.

'Peppy's into everything,' she whispered, thrusting her at him as soon as he arrived.

Peppy arched her back and squirmed to get down. 'Ssh,' he whispered, 'shh.' Peppy looked at him in surprise and reached up to pull his hair. 'Look,' he said, turning her round to watch, and jiggling her up and down on his knee.

His mum seemed awkward in this different dark kitchen, filling the kettle nervously, striking two matches to light the popping gas at the stove. The kettle clunked and hissed a little as she placed it over the flame.

'What did Lewis mean, keep me?'

She looked round surprised.

'Keep the boy,' he quoted.

'Finding enough room for us all to be together of course.' The basket of food she'd brought was on the wooden table. She unwrapped bread from a cloth and pulled a bit of crust off for Peppy. She cut two proper slices, and reached across for a plate from the dark oak dresser.

'Not those!'

Harry jumped. Peppy dropped her crust. Mrs Latcham stepped smartly through the door, snatched the plate away and passed an old chipped one from another pile. Surprisingly his mum said nothing. Instead she took another similar one and put a slice of bread on both. Looking over at Mrs Latcham, she took up the bread knife and hesitated over the loaf.

'I don't expect us to share anything,' said Mrs Latcham, glancing at the floor below Harry. He retrieved Peppy's soggy sucked crust and pushed it hopefully away across the table. Mum scooped it up, and produced a replacement. Peppy took that silently, playing with it now instead of chewing it, her nervous gaze fixed on Mrs Latcham. A steady fallout of crumbs rolled down onto the floor. Harry tried encouraging Peppy's hand towards her mouth.

His mum's hands were unsteady as she wrapped the bread up again. Out of the basket came a bowl of dripping. His favourite, the tastiest and brownest jelly part, was spread over one of the slices. The other slice was spread thinner, with more of the fat part on one half. She covered the bowl again, returned it to the basket but there was a grease mark on the wooden table where the dripping bowl had been.

Mrs Latcham glared at it. 'I must insist on cleanliness.'

Celia rubbed hard at the mark, but the grease stayed where it was. She took soap from the sink onto her cloth, and scrubbed again. The mark disappeared. But the yellow soap bar belonged to Mrs Latcham. Disapproval filled the air. Peppy burst into tears. 'Ssh!' Harry hissed, holding her tighter. 'Get down,' she shrieked, fretting and squirming.

'And quiet,' said Mrs Latcham.

Celia glared at Harry and took Peppy, bouncing her on her hip to silence her.

'I expect help in the house,' said Mrs Latcham, rearranging plates and cups slightly on the dresser as if they had been moved out of place. 'There are plenty of chores. As soon as you get a job, there's more rent to be paid. And you're to be out as much as possible.'

'Can we eat upstairs, Mum?'

'No meals upstairs,' said Mrs Latcham firmly.

'No,' said Celia, answering both. She pushed his plate towards him, the thick jelly spread bread one. Their eyes met. He saw the chance for solidarity, but instead he looked away.

Mrs Latcham glanced fiercely at him. 'He, of course, will be at school. I don't expect to find him in the house unnecessarily.' At the stove the kettle was nearly boiling. The whistle faltered right on the point of blowing, frilling along the edges of the blast to come.

'What about Saturdays and Sundays?' he pointed out. 'There's no school then.'

'I hope you're teaching your son manners and

not bringing him up to be impertinent, Mrs Beere,' said Mrs Latcham. The kettle whistled, shrill, full on.

His mum's hand was trembling as she turned the kettle off and, keeping Peppy well away, she poured boiling water onto the few tealeaves she'd put into Mrs Latcham's brown teapot. 'Sit up and be quiet, Harry,' she said.

He sat back, churning with anger, watching her put the teapot on the table, choose less than good cups from the dresser, and sit down herself with Peppy on her lap. 'Will you have some tea, Mrs Latcham?' The landlady shook her head.

A cup of weak tea, one slice of bread and dripping, with his mum sharing hers with Peppy, all eaten in silence. Some supper! And all with Mrs Latcham standing by the dresser in her dark shawl, watching.

Upstairs he sat on his made-up bed, playing angrily with a rubber band.

'Harry?'

He stayed where he was.

'I've made cocoa. The gas ring works but we'll have to watch Peppy with it.' She appeared in the doorway. 'We'll be fine,' she said, holding out a steaming cup. 'There's some of Amy's biscuits.

Want one?'

'Why are you going out, Mum?'

'Mr Cramer asked me. It was kind of him to drive us. To find this place.'

'And give you lipstick.'

'Don't be so silly.' She put his cocoa on the chest of drawers. 'Grown ups need time off. Time not to have to think about the war. I'm just going out for a drink.'

He watched her in the cracked wall mirror adjusting her hair so the missing bits of her comb didn't show. And putting on her new red lipstick. 'Peppy's asleep.' She pulled on her coat, bent down and straightened the seam on her new nylon stockings. 'No noise while I'm out now,' she said, leaning round the door. 'This is Mrs Latcham's home. Harry?'

He ignored her, stretching out the rubber band towards breaking point. She sighed, and came in to pull his blackout curtains closer. 'I won't be long.'

He flung himself back on the pillow as her footsteps retreated down the stairs. The front door closed. He snapped the rubber band between his fingers and then aimed it at the middle door.

He heard Mrs Latcham moving around

downstairs and lowered the rubber band. It wasn't his mum's fault they were here, but leaving his box behind, that was unforgivable. His clothes, all his precious beach stuff, the shells and things. Ones Daddy had found too. Worse, worst of all, the photograph. And now here she was going out with Lewis. He aimed again and let go. The rubber band hit the doorframe with a satisfying twang.

Chapter Nineteen

His dank little bedroom was still dark, but next door Mum had Peppy ready to go downstairs. Harry was hungry for breakfast himself.

It was dried egg omelette shared between them. Plum and swede jam on bread. Hot tea with powdered milk. Once they'd washed up and escaped upstairs, sponged and dressed Peppy, made the beds and tidied up, Mum said they must look for the market. With no garden to grow vegetables, and no friends with fruit trees, they would have to buy everything from now on. And be very careful with money. Peppy bounced on Harry's bed while he pulled on his snug new jumper and buttoned up his jacket.

Mrs Latcham's street led into the centre of town, right onto the market square. 'The River Dart is somewhere at the bottom of the hill,' Mum said cheerily.

The town was big. Stone houses, shops, and much bigger and busier than Harry expected, and full of agitated eyes, suspicious of strangers.

'Extra people of course,' Mum said, 'with so many like us arrived.'

'It's awful,' he said, thinking of the beach.

'It's a place to live,' she said.

All the market stalls had long queues. They joined one and waited. People stared at them. Harry wished the footsteps clattering on the cobbles were pebbles skittering in on the tide. The shouts of the traders echoing round the square might be seagulls screaming out over the bay. He wanted seaweed not damp air full of vegetable smells. Not fresh bread. Fish...

Peppy tugged him back to reality. He took her hand.

'A pound of apples please.' His mother counted out coins, checked her coupons. The greengrocer brought out apples from under the stall, weighed them, passed them to Harry while she paid. In the bag he counted five apples, two of them soft, mushy, rotten... A seagull screamed, right overhead.

'Mum?'

She looked, took the bag and gave it back. 'Could you replace the two bad ones please?'

The greengrocer tipped all the apples back into a box. 'Not good enough for you, lady?' He slung her money back into her hand. 'Try somewhere else.'

She gaped at him.

'Next?' he said, completely ignoring her.

She held out the money. 'But I'm paying!'

'Next!'

Harry felt his mother's shock and he could feel Peppy trying to break free from his grip, and see her face looking up at him in distress. People were elbowing in, pushing his mum out of the way. Celia put her arm round his rigid shoulders and pulled him aside. 'Come on.'

The anger burst out of him. 'Push his stall over!'

'Harry! What a thing! Then where would we be?' She prized Peppy's hand away from him, scanned the square. 'We're strangers here. Come on.'

Instead he skulked off on his own. He was calmer by the time he saw someone in another queue arguing with a butcher.

'How much? It can't be! How much are you saying?'

'Mrs Prouse?' At his call she swung round. How astonishing to find himself pleased to see her screwed-up angry face.

'Harry!'

'You want it, lady, or not?' demanded the butcher impatiently, holding up a scrawny rabbit. 'Plenty of others will buy it if you don't.' Mrs

Prouse turned back to business. 'How much?' But even she couldn't hold sway here. It was disappointing to see her meekly passing over the money. 'Frank's somewhere round,' she called after Harry.

He spotted him and moved fast. Hiding in a doorway he watched him confronting two boys, but Frank wasn't so certain here either. In the face of a shove from a united opposition, Frank backed off and returned to the protective company of his mother. She spoke to him and Frank scanned the square eagerly. Harry hid until they gave up looking.

On the far side of the square was a collection point for re-usable metal for the war effort and all sorts of other dusty old junk donated for the cause. His mum would never use things like torn curtains, and mouldy plates, but the people sorting through them sensed competition. They closed ranks and worked faster.

He wandered out into the High street. He could smell the river.

The quay was cold and deserted. There were old stone buildings sandbagged up, and more sandbags round a memorial to some explorer. Harry tried breathing on its marble surface, and writing his own name in the smear. It would be fun if one day there were monuments or books showing Harry Beere hiking up treacherous rock faces and huge mountains. Reaching the summit. Waving to cheering crowds. Exploring dangerous rivers, braving whirlpools, rushing waterfalls, swirling tides...

The river here wasn't much. Wide slippery mud banks. A central stream of dark water. Tidal, but not fresh and washed clean like his beach. A nice iron bridge spanned it though.

He stood in the centre looking down into the water, digging his tingling fingers deeper into his pockets for warmth, wishing he was on his beach. At the bottom of one pocket was a penny. Useful for that awful meter. Or Christmas. It was almost Christmas! In the other pocket was folded paper, and something gritty and sharp. He pulled them both out. The old map from the hide, and a shell! Pink fluted surface. Curled edge. Smooth and white and shiny inside. He dusted off a few stray grains of sand, polished it. Sniffed it for traces of the sea. He leaned over the rail, fiddling with it, thrilled to hold a tiny piece of sea magic. Suddenly it slipped away.

He snatched out wildly. The map fluttered off. The shell spun down like a tree seed. There was no splash as it hit the water and slid under the surface. He gripped the rail, wailing his distress down after it. His shout seemed to sink deep into the narrow stream and ebb away with the tide. A seagull rose screaming from the mud, and headed down river towards the coast.

Chapter Twenty

His mum was resting on her bed, eyes closed, pale. She'd had two days washing nappies in a bucket, and their clothes in the kitchen sink, and doing Mrs Latcham's washing as well, and the landlady's cleaning and ironing. And she'd been out looking for some kind of paid employment. Peppy was curled in beside her, asleep.

The old hawk had him cleaning too. Sweeping the yard. Scrubbing the lav floor. Washing the front door step. His fingers were red raw. Indoors he had to be quiet. Read or something, or play with Peppy. Seen, she said, only if absolutely necessary, and very definitely not heard. There was no school to escape to yet, and no boys he knew, not counting Frank of course. Outside in the cold, the choices were few. People, local kids, crossed the road avoiding strangers like him. He swung on the lamp post, sat in the gutter, walked the freezing streets, or just watched other kids playing.

The old hawk was out. No black coat hung on the downstairs hallstand. Curious, Harry pushed the door beside it, expecting it to groan on its hinges like a witch's door, but it swung open silently. The room had dark wooden picture rails, gloomy wallpaper, a fire grate with black mantel, with tiles up either side decorated with sombre lilies. A thin rug, patterned and dingy. An old upholstered chair in the corner, stiff and upright.

Against the nearest wall was a piano. Music here in Mrs Latcham's house? Harry lifted the dark polished lid, keen to finger the keys. He pushed one down slowly, softly so it didn't play. But she was out, wasn't she? He pressed harder. The note hung sweet and soft and mellow round him. He pressed it again. Then a higher one. He tried the first few notes of the twenty-third Psalm... How did it go? Daddy could play it. *The Lord's... The Lord's my shepherd...* Was that the tune? No, not quite right. He thought of old Mr Thorn in his box in the church. That was ages ago already. He tried again. The first notes, louder, hung on the air, quivered. He raised his eyes. From the wall a man in army uniform looked down. A young man. The photo was brown and unclear. But the eyes were strong, the eyebrows thick. A face, set and serious, as if trying to stay very still in time. A dark uniform, formal, straighter and tighter than Dad's. On the top of the piano, a black edged card, with lace on it, discoloured. Fine dust settled on his fingers as he opened it. Inside was another picture of the same man, in uniform again, and named in black lettering, William Wilber Latcham.

He heard a footfall outside in the street. A key sliding into the lock. Heart pounding, he placed the card back, shut the piano lid and slid back out into the hall. No time to escape upstairs, or into the kitchen. He shot his hand down inside the umbrella bucket on the hallstand just as the door opened and Mrs Latcham entered. He looked up innocently at her. 'Our umbrella?' he said.

She narrowed her eyes at him. Sniffed at the steam from the washing drying in the kitchen. Glanced at the parlour door. Was it open a little too wide?

'Are you snooping, Harry Beere?'

He drew back.

She folded her own umbrella and added it to the hallstand. 'Stealing perhaps?' She took off her coat and hung it up. She pulled out her long sharp hatpin and removed her black hat. Her black jacket clung in round her waist. Her skirt was narrow and black. Even her shoes were black. More than hawk now. A spider ready to jump. 'Were you in my parlour?'

He pressed back hard against the wall hearing

his mum move out onto the landing above.

Mrs Latcham heard her too, but she spoke loudly and directly to him. 'My quarters are my own,' she said. 'Private and not to be entered under any circumstances. Inform your mother immediately she must find somewhere else to stay.'

Celia scuttled down the stairs. 'Mrs Latcham, please! Look, I have some rent for you.'

Mrs Latcham snatched the money and counted it. 'This isn't enough,' she said.

'Lewis… Mr Cramer's promised to help me with it this week,' she pleaded.

A flash of disapproval crossed the hawk's face. 'I hope you're not planning to entertain Lewis Cramer in my house!'

'No! Of course not! Oh, Mrs Latcham, please let us stay.'

Harry prayed the old hawk's thin lips would say no. No. No! You leave now! But when he glanced back at his mother's frightened face, he suddenly dreaded what might be said. For a fearful moment Mrs Latcham considered, then her mouth tightened and she tucked the money down her front.

Celia stepped back nervously. 'It's Christmas Eve tomorrow, Mrs Latcham. I wondered… Will you be…'

Mrs Latcham glared at her. 'I would be grateful,' she said coldly, 'if you would keep the noise to a minimum. Christmas is not a time for disturbance.'

'May I cook a meal?'

'You may use the kitchen as you normally do. I will be out.' And she swept away down the dark hall to her room behind the stairs.

Chapter Twenty One

The Priory Church of St Mary had a Christmas tree, candles on the altar, and masses of familiar carols to sing as well as the hymns. There was ice on the protective tape on the inside of the stained glass windows, but in spite of the freezing cold, the pews were full.

Harry's mum nudged him and smiled. 'Lovely, isn't it,' she whispered. She held Peppy up. 'Look!' She pointed to some other little children down the front, all pink-cheeked and rugged up in red scarves. It was comforting to be here, Harry decided, cheerful that people wanted to be together, though things weren't shaping up at all well back at Mrs Latcham's.

Somewhere behind them someone whispered, 'Got that Warden for a boyfriend, hasn't she?' Harry swung round, but people were opening their hymnbooks. 'Pays for her...' *Oh come all ye faithful, joyful and...*'That little dictator?' Still Harry couldn't see who was saying such things *... come ye to Bethlehem...*

Maybe Mum hadn't heard. On the way in he'd seen a couple of men smiling at her, and women looking away as if she was some kind of threat. Now there was a big gap between her and the next person, as if no one wanted to sit too close. She was a whole lot prettier than those other women. Listening to her singing, her voice as clear and strong as it had always been, he worried she looked different now, sadder since they'd left home. Her hat, her only one, was at a strange angle and Lewis's red lipstick on her lips looked a bit too bright.

When the collection came round, she hugged Peppy to her, carefully avoiding the plate, making Harry reach along and pass it on. Once it was gone by, she nudged him and opened her palm to reveal she'd kept back the two shiny pennies. 'Better in the meter, don't you think?' she whispered.

The final hymn was specially chosen, the vicar said, '...to give a warm welcome to our Allies. And to let us remember as we go towards 1944, the fifth year of this terrible war, how hard and bravely we are all fighting. Let us sing from our hearts.'

Organ and voices burst upwards, echoing into the rafters, like musical waves, pounding across the vaulted roof... *Onward Christian soldiers, marching as to war...*

Harry wondered if people were singing from their hearts? Did they really want their soldiers marching onward? The cross going in front of them was very worrying. Near him in a dark corner, lit by rows of small white candles, was a cross. Below it, carved into pink marble, were long lists of names of men in the First World War who had never come home.

When they sat back after the prayers, he whispered, 'Mum, why doesn't Dad write? Where is he?'

Peppy looked up at her too. Celia turned the pages of the prayer book back and forth nervously. 'I'm not sure,' she whispered. 'He's missing, isn't he, so no one knows.'

'Will he know where we are?'

She didn't seem to know that either. Instead she got out her handkerchief and wiped Peppy's nose, and nudged Harry to stand up with her for the next Christmas carol.

Peppy was fast asleep on her shoulder as they filed out after the service. No one looked at them or spoke to them as they left. 'We're new of course,' Mum whispered. 'Strangers in town.'

But Harry wondered, remembering the whispers earlier, if her going out with Lewis wasn't the real problem.

The night air was crisp and freezing. Walking back through the silent streets to Mrs Latcham's, their breath steamed out in front of them. Ice crunched under their shoes. The scattering of stars above looked like little white diamonds, pinpricks sparkling in a great arc of darkness.

'Do you think Daddy can see these stars too?' he asked.

His mum pulled her coat closer round Peppy and looked up. 'Harry, it's Christmas.'

Chapter Twenty Two

Harry pulled his new knitted socks higher and leaned back in his chair. It had been a good day, and for once they could be sure of having the kitchen to themselves. It was toasting warm and still smelt deliciously of roast meat. The bones of the scrawny chicken lay on the chipped dish, next to an empty tin with a picture of golden pineapple on it, and three silver paper chocolate wrappers.

Celia examined the china shepherdess all over again.

'I got it from the fund raising. In the market.'

'It's wonderful, Harry. Thank you.' She placed it on the table and he watched her fingering the lacy edge, and moving it around this way and that to get a better view. She didn't seem to see it was chipped. He was pleased now he'd spent his penny on it.

'Wish we were back home.' Strange today, not the beach but thoughts of his old bedroom nagged at him. The cosy kitchen. The old lav outside, a hundred times better than here. The old tin tub they hauled in every Saturday night, put in front the fire and filled with water boiled up in the kitchen copper. 'Think of the bath.'

'Ooh yes!' Celia shut her eyes.

'All warm and soapy.'

'You first, me, then Daddy.'

'Then hot tea by the fire before bed.'

'Us laughing and talking.'

Yes, he thought, us all laughing and talking. You and Daddy.

She was smiling. 'Not the...'

'Not the Ritz...' Daddy said it all the time, 'not the Ritz, but ours.'

Peppy smiled up at them, her cheeks covered in chocolate. She drummed the wooden spoon hard against her new cardboard box house.

Celia laughed and reached up in a long, lazy arm stretch. 'She loves her box, Harry. Clever you, finding it.' She dipped suddenly into her pocket. 'Look!' she said eagerly. 'A US dollar.' It was flat and round and silver in her palm.

Harry glanced away.

'Lewis gave it to me! And wasn't it nice of him to send us all this food?'

'Weird, isn't it, how he had all those tins of pineapple? Is Lewis what they call a spiv?'

She moved the tin defensively. 'It's one tin!'

'Well, you only got one of them.'

She stiffened. 'What?'

He wished desperately he hadn't disturbed the atmosphere of peace and goodwill. 'Nothing.'

'What?' she demanded.

There was no way out now. 'There were more.'

Celia frowned, disbelieving him again. 'Don't be silly.'

His punctured pride made him leap up and throw open Mrs Latcham's store cupboard. Inside was proof: a stack of tins of pineapple and beside them, tins of corned beef. 'I saw him bring them in.'

Celia stared at them. 'It might have been towards the rent,' she said. 'Or to convince her to let us stay,' she added, less certainly.

'Or even her being really mean.' He bit his lip. He hadn't meant to say that either. It made Lewis look good.

The front door opened. He shut the cupboard fast and sat down. The old hawk appeared, glancing immediately at the dirty plates and the pineapple tin. She stood there in silence, drawing that lethal hatpin from her hat very slowly.

Celia snatched up the pineapple tin and leapt to her feet to clear the table. Harry rose too, in solidarity. Peppy ducked down inside her box.

'Happy Christmas, Mrs Latcham,' Celia said,

scraping the chicken bones into a saucepan, and pouring hot water from the kettle on them. She emptied the rest of the boiled water into the sink and set about washing up. 'Have you had a good day?'

Mrs Latcham sniffed. No 'Happy Christmas' back. 'I'm surprised you don't take advantage of your own relatives' hospitality this Christmas, Mrs Beere, instead of using my house.'

The old chipped chicken plate slid out of Celia's grasp into the washing up. As she pulled it out, dripping, it split in half in her hands. She stared at it in horror. 'Oh, I'm so sorry.'

Mrs Latcham held her hat up like a trophy and speared it with the hatpin. 'Damage now,' she said. 'Of course, maybe you weren't invited anywhere. There's probably quite an element of disapproval.'

'What?' said Celia softly. A blush of pink rose up her neck.

'Not everyone is as generous as I am.'

Harry couldn't bear it any longer. 'We were asked, weren't we, Mum!' he shouted. 'We've got relations!'

'Well!' said Mrs Latcham. 'If you do have accommodation elsewhere you can…'

'Harry! Hold your tongue!' cried Celia. He'd

never seen her look so frightened.

Why did she always take everyone else's side? Why wasn't she shouting back at this rude woman? 'But we will, won't we, Mum!' he begged. 'We will go!'

On the verge of tears, Celia turned submissively to Mrs Latcham. 'We have no relations, Mrs Latcham. There's nowhere else we can go.' She grabbed Peppy up and left the room.

Mrs Latcham narrowed her eyes at Harry. 'So. Telling lies now!'

Hawk? Mrs Latcham was a witch! He grabbed up the china shepherdess and Peppy's box and struggled up the stairs.

Chapter Twenty Three

He sat on the floor near Peppy's cardboard house, with the orange, the bar of chocolate, and the warm second-hand scarf he'd been given. He tore the wrapping off the chocolate. Peppy could have it. He didn't want to eat it.

Behind him the National Anthem was playing softly. The last thing he wanted to do was look round, but he chanced it. Mum was sitting next to the wireless tearfully trying to fit pieces of cardboard into the split soles of his shoes.

'She can swing for the washing up,' she muttered.

'Mum, can Peppy have...?'

'Ssh!' she said, turning up the volume on the wireless. 'It's the King.'

And it was.

'To many of you my... words will come as you sit in the quiet of your homes. But wherever you may be, today, of all days of the year, your thoughts... will be in distant places and your hearts with those you love.'

Harry held the chocolate over the edge of the box. A little hand reached up for it.

'I hope that my words, spoken to them and to you,

may be the bond that joins us all in company for a few moments on this Christmas day...to all those on service good luck and a stout heart; to all who wait for them to ...return, proud memories and high hopes to keep you strong; to all children, here and in the lands beyond the seas, a day of real happiness.'

'Mum, why did you say we've got nobody? What about Grandma?'

'What about me?' Celia dropped the shoe she working on into her lap and put her head in her hands. 'What am I supposed to do? Bombs fall, Harry. My family gets killed. My mother. I can't just dream new relations up.'

He got to his feet and left the broadcast behind to stare out the window trying hard to remember the time before Daddy went away, when his grandma came to stay.

'She walked on the beach with me.'

Distantly the King's voice continued, a hesitant, faltering sort of voice, sounding unsure in spite of the brave words. *'We know that much hard working and hard fighting, and perhaps harder working and harder fighting than ever before, are necessary for victory. We shall not rest from our task until it is nobly ended...'*

'Remember the bomb falling on the thatched cottage?' Celia said.

148

'Yes.'

'They'd been bombing Plymouth that night. My mother's house took a direct hit.'

He swung round. 'You didn't tell me! You were crying! I thought it was about Daddy going away.'

'It was. It was about… everything.'

'Why didn't you tell me?'

'There was enough to think about next day with your father joining up.'

'Will Daddy have Christmas?'

Celia stared at the floor. 'He went to war to fight for us, Harry. So we might live in a safer world.'

'He's never met Peppy. And she hardly talks anymore. She used to be a chatterbox.'

He watched Celia's hands gripping together so that the knuckles were white. 'She's upset, like we all are.'

'You didn't go back for my box.'

'What?'

'You left it behind.'

'I couldn't go back. How could we go back?'

'You could have made him.' He ran his fingers along the windowsill. Somewhere out in the street he could hear people singing. 'What about Daddy's family?'

'Coventry. But you knew that.'

The singing faded into the distance. 'Are they buried?'

Celia abandoned the shoes onto the floor, started to tidy up the room and make the bed. 'Where they lived was…' her voice had a break in it, 'there was nothing left.'

The King's voice filled the empty space. *'From this ancient and beloved festival that we are keeping, sacred as it is to home and all that home means, we can draw strength to face the future of a world driven by a tempest such as it has never endured. In the words of a Scottish writer of our day: "No experience can be too strange and no task too formidable, if a man can link it up with what he knows and loves."'*

Harry watched her lift Peppy out of the box. 'Lewis wants me to go out for a quick drink later. You'll be all right.'

He turned away from her and stared down into the dark deserted street. 'But you won't know where we are,' he whispered.

Chapter Twenty Four

The railway station was busy. Crowds of GIs and British soldiers milled round the entrance, their hot breath misting the morning air. Harry tugged the sleeve of a GI. The fresh-faced marine listened earnestly. 'What's his outfit?'

'Second Battalion. In Italy I think?'

'Sorry, pal.'

The next GI didn't know either. Nor did the next.

A British soldier patted him on the shoulder as another GI shrugged and moved away into the crowd. 'Never been to Italy, any of them, lad. Fresh off the old US of A. cherry tree, they are. Wouldn't know a Jerry if they saw one!' The soldier thought about it but he didn't know either.

Someone must know. There must be some way to find out. A shrill whistle streaked through the cold crisp air. Harry pushed his way out onto the crowded platform as another train hissed into the station. People pulled back from the edge. And just before he stepped back himself, at the very far end of the platform he thought he saw...

The engine shunted past. Inside the cab, a grimy fireman shovelled coal into the hungry engine. Black smoke shimmered from the stack, and white steam belched up from the wheels.

He ran fast, pushing his way past soldiers, women in hats, people with cases and trunks. Coats. Bicycles. Mailbags. The guard jostling his way through.

The train shuddered to a halt.

'Hi! Hi!' he shouted, over the screech of metal wheels.

'The kid from the beach!' Mike grinned. 'So you're here!' But his focus was already on carriage windows sliding down, people reaching out to click the locks. Doors banging open. He moved briskly away along the crowded platform.

Harry ran to keep up with him. 'What's happening back in Torcross?'

'Torcross, Totnes. You guys sure have confusing town names! You and your mom settling in?'

'Landlady's a real witch!'

Mike dodged round GIs shouldering kitbags and pulling on metal helmets. 'How come you're here at the station, kid?'

'I'm looking for my dad. He's missing and we still haven't had any letters. He'll come home to the beach. Now we've moved, how will he know where we are?'

Mike halted in his tracks and looked at him.

'Can you look in my house? Can you see if there are any letters?'

Mike was staring at him.

'What?'

There was an impatient shout from further along.

'What, GI?'

Mike hesitated for a moment longer. Then he fished in his pocket and thrust a handful of chocolate bars at Harry. 'Been saving these in case I saw you,' he said. He ruffled Harry's hair and sprinted off towards a group of senior officers alighting from the end of the train. And then he was gone, disappeared into the throng of more GIs streaming off the train.

Lines of soldiers closed in round Harry, taking over the station, shutting out the light. Steam. Shouting. Shoving. It felt like being swallowed up.

Chapter Twenty Five

'You can mind her this afternoon, can't you, Harry?'

In the corner on the floor Peppy leaned in on him like a purring little kitten. Her eyes focussed on the picture he was drawing for her. A silly face. A smiley one. Then another one with a wiggly mouth. He drew a house with doors and windows and a sun in the sky. As soon as each picture was done, she wanted another.

'That greengrocer turned me down again.' In front of the cracked mirror Celia was trying on her felt hat. It made her look like a school kid. And thin. Worryingly skinny under her slip. 'Don't think he likes strangers invading his town or shopping at his stall.'

'Are we strangers?'

'I suppose we are.'

'But we're English, aren't we?'

Laid out on her bed was the green tweed suit and maroon sweater the WVS lady had delivered. Harry drew a stick figure while she put it on. Peppy rubbed her finger over the picture. 'Mummy?'

'So? What do you think?'

He shrugged, wishing the green skirt and purple sweater were something prettier.

'It's a start. Maybe voluntary work will be fun. Lewis keeps telling me to be more cheerful.'

Lewis? Who cared about Lewis! Before he could say so, the door burst open. He could see his mum was shocked Mrs Latcham hadn't knocked. Quite right! These rooms were theirs. Paid for. Private and not to be entered under any circumstances.

The old hawk hadn't noticed him. He pressed himself back into the corner. Peppy copied him. Celia moved swiftly, taking hold of the door handle, limiting the access. 'Yes?'

For once the landlady looked her up and down approvingly. She nodded at the purple sweater. 'My husband liked that colour,' she said. Her bony fingers reached out and felt the wool. Her expression softened. For a moment it was possible to believe the person in front of his mum was might have feelings.

'Your husband?'

'A soldier, like yours,' said Mrs Latcham softly. 'Today's his birthday.'

Harry frowned, seeing his mum's confusion too. Was there a man living somewhere in the house? Had they missed that?

'Just twenty-three,' said Mrs Latcham, 'when he went over the top.'

'Oh,' said Celia gently. 'The last war.'

Mrs Latcham glanced around and saw the shepherdess ornament on the chest of drawers. 'What's that?'

Celia smiled and stepped back a little, allowing a better view. 'Isn't it pretty?'

Mrs Latcham blinked. She snapped her shawl closer round her shoulders. 'I am very particular,' she said, stepping in past Celia and reverting to her normal irritable tone, 'about what's on show in my house, Mrs Beere. Please don't add your own taste.'

Celia picked up the ornament protectively. 'Harry gave it to me,' she said. He saw her glance down at the shepherdess, noticing for the first time there was a chip in the porcelain.

'If you have spare money,' said Mrs Latcham, 'I would be grateful if you would pay your way more clearly here. Are you taking the boy to the dairy?'

'Tomorrow.'

'Good. Less time spent in my house.'

Harry jumped to his feet. 'What dairy?'

Mrs Latcham registered his appearance and

sudden outburst with distaste, as if it exactly proved her point.

'As Mr Cramer says, it's quite time you put the boy out to work!'

'What dairy?'

'We'll discuss it later.'

'Mum?'

'Quiet!'

Harry pushed past them both, skittered down the stairs and out, slamming the front door after him.

Chapter Twenty Six

With no jacket, walking fast was the only way to keep warm. The watery lunchtime sun drew him up to the fields above the town. Soon he ran, exhilarated by the space, the light, the clear air. He raced over the ridge, arms stretched wide like a fighter plane. Seagulls, feeding in new ploughed earth, rose up in alarm. It was satisfying, scaring them into flight. Above him now they formed his squadron, flying with him. He circled and dipped. They followed. He banked round against the glinting sun and turned like the Spitfires on the newsreels. Making best use of the glare behind him, he set his sights on the boundary hedge on the end of the field. He zoomed in.

Something moved inside the target range. Something in shadow, beyond the hedge. He was gaining ground, and recognising all at once. The figure emerging began to run menacingly towards him with a droning sound like a fighter plane, shooting directly at him.

'Ak, ak, ak, ak, ak...'

Harry ran faster and faster. At the last moment

he dipped joyfully and arched away. He felt as if he would burst with delight. He cut back, and took up the challenge again. The two of them chased each other breathlessly, doubling back across and round the edges of the field. When Harry nearly had him, the foe always managed to scoot away. Eventually they drew level and came in to land, throwing themselves down on the damp grass panting and laughing.

'Shot you down five times over, Harry Beere.'

'Rubbish!' he breathed, grinning at the familiar grubby short trousers, floppy cap and frayed red scarf, at the boy who could climb trees faster than anyone.

Tim grinned. 'You here in town?'

'Yep! You?'

'Now we are.'

'Where did you go?'

'Way inland first. But there was nowhere for Lillie and me. Dad's doing all sorts here, but at least we're together. You?'

'Rooming with a real witch. Peppy, me and Mum! The Warden found it for her.'

'Lewis Cramer?' Tim glowered. 'He took his belt to our Lillie when he found her at the station first day we were back. She's still got the mark.'

Harry gasped.

'When Dad complained, Lewis reckoned he only smacked her for giving cheek, but she doesn't tell fibs.'

'You know the photo of my dad? It got left behind and Lewis wouldn't let us go back for it.'

'Your mum still...' Tim stopped. He rolled onto his back and gazed up at the sky.

Harry stared angrily up at the sky too. 'Something awful might happen. I think. One day.'

An ominous silence stretched out between them. The air temperature was falling.

Tim thumped him cheerfully on the chest. 'C'mon, I'm thirsty!'

Two cows calmly munching feed looked round as the boys crept into the barn on the hill nearby.

'Guard the door,' Tim said. He poked about and found two old buckets. 'Wrong time of day, but there'll be some,' he whispered. He slid one bucket underneath one of the cows, and turned the other bucket upside down to sit on. She went on pulling and snuffling through the hayrack in front of her.

'Watch out for cow pats,' Harry whispered.

Tim yelped with laughter.

'Ssh!'

Carefully Tim reached in towards her udder. She twitched, shifted a foot, settled again. Soon there were rhythmical squirts of fresh milk foaming into the metal bucket below. Tim looked up. 'Your turn, Harry.'

It was hard, leaning in under the cow's weight, pulling the warm teats down.

'Haven't you ever done it?'

'No.' It was strange, the feel of her warm damp skin in his hand. Keeping the rhythm was difficult, and her hide twitched whenever he lost his timing.

'Got to learn to move quiet round them,' whispered Tim. 'Quiet as a snake. And quieter 'n that.'

Afterwards they sat on bales of hay, laughing and joking, dipping into the warm, frothy milk with cupped hands and drinking eagerly. Nothing had ever tasted so delicious.

'Hen house next,' suggested Tim.

After a terrible lot of squawking, and flying feathers, they emerged laughing and triumphant, with one egg each.

'Oi!'

'It's the farmer!'

'You leave them chickens!' he yelled, bristling

down the lane towards them waving a shotgun. 'I be after you! Young scallywags!'

They ran. A shot rang out. They scooted faster down the hill towards a stile, breathing hard, laughing and falling over each other to climb over it fast.

'Quick,' cried Tim, glancing back. 'He's taking aim!'

Across the field, barbed wire stuck up from a low hedge as Harry sprinted behind Tim towards it. Bang! A shot whistled over his head. Tim vaulted nimbly over the hedge and disappeared. Harry leapt too but not high enough. The wire caught him, ripping in behind his knee. He dropped painfully into the ditch on the other side, breathing fast, feeling instantly sick. He grabbed his stinging leg. His fingers were covered with blood.

Tim was back beside him in a second. He glanced nervously at the gash and risked a look back over the hedge. 'It's all right. Farmer's given up. Too old for the chase. You all right?'

The cut was smarting and Harry felt shaky but he wasn't going to say so. He reached into his pocket and pulled out broken egg. 'Thanks!' he said, thrusting the gooey handful at Tim.

Tim laughed, ducking away. The egg mess fell

on the earth and dribbled away. He examined Harry's bleeding leg anxiously. 'Can you stand?'

'Course I can!'

'The river. C'mon.'

With Tim's help Harry limped down the steep stony hill to the riverbank.

'Handkerchief?'

Harry dug it out.

'Could make a tourniquet, but the bleeding's stopped.' Instead Tim dipped it into the water. 'First rule of combat injury. Clean the wound!' He bathed the cut carefully, eventually using his own handkerchief as well, making quite a good tight bandage. 'Can you get home?'

'Course!'

Chapter Twenty Seven

Harry closed the front door quietly. He was almost to the top when light from the kitchen streaked across the staircase. 'You're too late for your mother to cook you any supper.'

'Mum?' he called up towards the rooms.

'She's out,' the old hawk said, glaring up at him. She caught sight of his bandaged leg. 'You've been fighting!'

Harry escaped into his bedroom and closed the door. Her voice floated up the stairs after him. 'Your mother expected you here.'

In his mother's room the purple sweater was discarded on her bed. Her hairbrush and the red lipstick too. But no Peppy. He ran back down the stairs in spite of his leg.

Peppy was in the kitchen with Mrs Latcham, kicking against the legs of her chair, her little cheeks flushed scarlet.

'Where were you?' demanded Mrs Latcham.

Harry snatched Peppy up. She dug her head deep into his neck. 'It's all right,' he whispered, 'you're all right. You're with me.' Upstairs he put her on his bed and dug under the mattress for one of Mike's chocolate bars. Even though he was always starving hungry, he'd kept these for real emergencies. Right now Peppy badly needed cheering up. 'Half each?' Peppy stared at his bandaged leg. 'Just a scratch,' he said, unwrapping the chocolate bar.

He propped her up with pillows and sat with his arm round her, eating his half slowly, savouring the welcome sweetness, angry his mother was out again.

'All right, Pep?' He gave her a squeeze. 'Go on, say something.'

She raised her eyes to him, but went on sucking the chocolate bar.

He moved in closer to comfort her. 'Remember Tim? I saw him today up in the fields...'

He heard a car door and his mother's voice. He hurried through to the other window. Below in the dark street Lewis was leaning in close. Too close. 'You leave my mum alone!'

Lewis looked up, furious. Her too. She pulled away and opened the front door. Harry stayed at the window enjoying Lewis's anger, watching him climb into his jeep and accelerate away.

Celia burst into the room. She seemed excited, glowing. Her eyes were bright, but she shouted at him angrily. 'How dare you stay out so late!'

'You left Peppy with the hawk!'

'Where were you?'

'I'm not going to any old dairy!'

'It's all set up, Harry.'

The sweet aftertaste of chocolate stuck in Harry's throat. Peppy was crying. He couldn't say he'd seen Tim, or what a good day it had been. Lewis was in her head. There was nothing to do but pass Peppy through, shut the communicating door and go to bed.

Dust glittered in the shaft of light from the whirring projector at the back of the cinema.

'You won't see him,' Tim whispered.

Harry leaned forward, concentrating on the faces on the screen. Some men rested shyly on their rifles. One clowned around for the camera. Others put cigarettes nervously to their lips. They all looked dusty and tired and thin.

'If he's missing, how would he be in the picture? Anyway missing means...'

Harry stared hard at the flickering black and white pictures searching for the slightest recognisable turn of a head. The familiar smile. Then in a flash all the British soldiers were gone. Instead smartly dressed GIs lurched down gangplanks from troop carriers to scratchy, happy music. The crowds on the newsreel was cheering and waving.

It was said there was good news, that the tide of war might be turning, but nobody dared believe it. There were rumours of a Second Front. Harry heard people say it would start in the Balkans, or Norway. If more troops went to Italy, might Dad be found?

Tim around made things more cheerful. School had started, after a fashion, and though Ernie the milkman warned Harry to behave or else, helping on the milk round was a nifty little job. It meant starting early, before it was light, but then the chore would be easily out of the way before school. It earned him a drink of milk every day and one shilling and sixpence on Saturdays. The milk stopped him feeling so hungry, and it felt good to have something responsible to do, and money to help his mum feed Mrs Latcham's hungry meters, or buy the tap for them all to have a bath.

Ernie was cheery, and chatted on the doorsteps as he went. At particular houses he disappeared inside. Customer service he called it. Harry held the horse and waited, but some doorsteps he did himself. People took their milk, paid, and as they began to get to know him, just sometimes they told him to keep the penny change.

Chapter Twenty Eight

'Does he wear jackboots?'

Tim ran ahead. 'Let's see.' Harry chased him. They were both out of breath when they reached the farm on the hill.

'Side lane?' Tim suggested. 'Dad steers clear of the old boy who owns this land. Pays mean wages and has a filthy temper.'

They crawled under a hedge, and jumped a ditch. There was a woodpile against the wall ahead. They climbed carefully, fearful of dislodging the logs. From the top they looked down on a cobbled yard and the stone tiled roof of a pigsty.

A blonde lad was shovelling manure into a wheelbarrow. He saw them, they could tell, but he went on with his work. He looked older than they were, mouse poor and scarecrow thin. Except for his open jacket, everything else he wore was muddy and torn, and loose. A piece of string round his waist held his trousers up.

'Go on! Speak German then!' Tim called down.

Below them the lad concentrated harder on his shovelling.

'Nothing different about him except his ragged clothes. Let's go.'

'Wait!' whispered Tim. He pointed over at the sty. 'Any piglets?' he called. The lad glanced round nervously before he looked up at them.

Tim grinned. 'There's only us. I'm Tim. He's Harry.'

'What's your name?' asked Harry.

'I am August.'

'See?' whispered Tim. 'Who has a funny name like that here?'

August glanced round again, and put down his shovel. 'I show you big pig and her little ones?' He pushed a barrel over to the wall.

They clambered down into the yard and he turned to lead the way. On the back of his jacket was the tell tale patch in shocking bright yellow. Prisoner of war. 'Meaning this person has been captured, and brought here to work.' whispered Tim. 'Danger! Stay alert! Enemy! Do not fraternise!'

August's thin arm reached up for the catch on the sty door. Harry stared at the frayed string ends hanging down from the boy's skinny waist, and the rough, worn out boots. Was this the fighting image on the newsreels? The imagined enemy in their games?

August pulled the old door open and turned to see if they were following. 'You come?'

'How many piglets are there?' asked Tim, ducking inside.

Harry wanted to say something, ask things. Instead he followed August in, a heavy hollow silence growing inside his head.

The sow lay in the warm, pungent, pig-smelling place, snuffling her nose into the loose hay around her. Her six babies scrabbled and struggled, squeaking round her, fighting each other to feed. August leaned down for one of them and passed it to Harry. His hands were all skin and bone. 'You have bread maybe?' he asked.

'No, sorry,' Harry said, really wishing he had. The piglet squirmed and snuffled in his arms. He stroked its smooth pink baby skin and let it suck hard at his finger. It had fine, pale eyelashes.

'Are you a prisoner of war?' asked Tim, rubbing at the old metal on the feed bucket.

'I am from Ansbach, yes?' He held out his arms for the piglet. He took it gently and petted its floppy ears.

'Why are you here?'

August put the little pig down by its mother, pushing another away to give this smaller one a chance to feed. He straightened up and shrugged. 'I help my father on our farm. We build good house to live in. War comes. He has to leave to fight for my country.'

'The enemy,' nodded Tim.

August turned on him. 'Why is enemy?'

'My father is away fighting,' Harry said.

August bit his lip. 'Farm is finish. I do not know where my father goes. Poland? To the Russian Front? Now I am prisoner.'

'Where's your mother?'

August shook his head sadly. The sound of a tractor rattled up the field. He turned pale. 'Go! Quick! Quick!'

They were over the wall and away before the tractor reached the top of the hill.

'You can't trust them,' said Tim. 'There's a war on.'

'We'll go back,' Harry said. 'We'll take him food.'

When they climbed the woodpile beside the wall two days later, a local boy was tending the pigs.

'Clear off!' he called. 'Farmer warned me you kids were hanging round.'

'Where's August?' Harry asked. The boy looked at him as if he was mad.

'He was here, working with the pigs,' explained Tim.

The boy shrugged. 'Been moved, I s'pose,' he said. 'Like all them prisoners.'

When Harry told her, his mum seemed pleased to hear any prisoners of war had been moved away.

'But he's only a farmer's son.'

'It's dangerous having any of them round here,' said Celia. 'Lewis says it's dangerous.'

It was Frank who was dangerous. Kicking a football round the school yard became a full on fight with anyone who dared challenge him. Harry tried, but Frank would bring him down and kick him in the ribs. And if he got possession in a proper game, Frank would put the boot in afterwards.

'The devil take the enemy!' cried Miss Rosewall, reporting a daytime air raid on a school near London. 'A Midsummer Night's Dream those poor little girls were watching. All dead in the bombs.'

Harry's inkwell, like the water in the pipes, was frozen solid so he couldn't write down Miss Rosewall's instructions for what to do in the event of an air raid at this school. He was shivering, his fingers too cold to write. All she said was: 'Take shelter! And keep down!' And you would keep down if the sky was full of bombs, wouldn't you? He bet the little girls had.

Miss Rosewall held up newspaper pictures of the King and Queen inspecting bomb damage, and the one of St Paul's cathedral in London rising out of the devastation around it, and more buildings half fallen down.

'We're bombing them now like they bombed us, and the Russians are victorious!' Miss Rosewall proclaimed. 'We have to stick together. The tide of the war is turning. Listen to Mr Churchill!'

The hour of our greatest effort and action is approaching. The magnificent armies of the United States are pouring in. Our own troops, the best trained and best equipped we have ever had, stand at their side in equal numbers and in comradeship.

Chapter Twenty Nine

Harry lay on the riverbank, staring up at the first evening star. Daddy always said when spring was on the way he could smell it. Somewhere down in the dark below new shoots sensed the daylight hours lengthening. Harry breathed in. The winter mustiness in the ground under him was gone. There was a sprouting sweetness deep in the earth, like some distant promise of new cut hay on a summer wind.

Water was pouring over the waterfall, a line of rocks forming a natural crossing over the river when the tide was out. It was going out now.

'If Mum had the photo she'd remember Dad. She wouldn't go out with that creep Lewis then.'

Tim was messing about with a stick in the shallows. He gazed out across the river. 'We ain't got a picture of our mum.' He threw the stick aside and stepped out onto the first stone in the crossing. 'But Dad says Lillie's the spitting image. Just as well since she killed her.'

Harry sat up. 'What?'

'Mum died having her.'

'You never told me that!'

Tim balanced on one leg. 'You never asked.'

'Do you miss her?'

Tim balanced carefully on the other leg. 'Can't remember much except what Dad tells us.' He glanced across cheekily. 'Dare you!' Sure footed as ever, he skipped nimbly across to the other side of the river.

Harry leapt up, afraid of being left behind, and wondering if Mum would ever tell Peppy about Daddy? He teetered across the wet rocks, scared with every step he'd slip into the gushing water below.

'My poor little Lill,' Tim went on when Harry reached him. 'Did her mother in, and broke her father's heart. I got to look after her.'

'I thought Miss Rosewall was. Lewis said...' He stopped, bit his lip. Last night he'd heard Lewis in his mother's room talking about contacting the authorities.

'Only out of school hours. Anyway what would stupid Lewis know?' He picked up a stone and threw it into the water. 'Still no letter from your dad then?'

'No.' Harry threw a stone himself and looked round for another. It was getting dark. 'Mum never mentions him now. And she cries and says the WVS ladies don't speak to her.'

'Bet that's because of Lewis.'

'Hear the explosions last night?'

'Wind was blowing in from the coast, that's why. Dad says the farmers all talk now about needing passes to move round their own land.'

'What's it all mean?'

Tim shrugged. 'Invasion?'

'With all those GIs there?'

'Maybe that's why they wanted us out.' He chucked a stone up into the branches of a huge tree. It brushed through the high leaves. Tim dodged as it dropped back to the ground. 'Reckon we could climb this?'

'No!'

'I will. Bet you! Tomorrow.'

'Tomorrow's school.'

A tiny glimmer of light drew them further along the riverbank. Closer, they heard a swish, a plop. A whirring sound.

'Fish!' Tim whispered.

'Fish?'

'Ssh! C'mon.'

They crept along under the bushes. The sound of water gushing behind them was replaced by a man's humming ahead. They couched down, watching. He sat facing the dark water, concentrating, or dreaming. Behind him on the ground were two shiny fat fish.

'Bet you can't get them,' whispered Tim. Harry drew back. 'Go on, fraidy!'

Harry took a deep breath and crawled forward. The man shifted on the ground, lit up a cigar. The flume of match light showed military buttons. A GI, and at this moment unaware, but maybe only briefly. The slightest sound and he'd know someone was behind him. He started to hum a new tune. Harry was close now, within reach. He could almost smell the fish cooking in a pan, and taste the salty lick of the white flesh. Back in the bushes Tim nodded encouragement.

The GI's hum continued as he began winding in his line. Heart pounding, Harry reached out. The whirring noise covered the slipping and sliding sound of the fish coming towards him over the grass. He grasped them close smelling the dank dark river in them, and inched backwards across the ground etching a pattern in the loose earth. The winding stopped. The humming ended. A night owl flapped up and flew away, its wings creaking. Then there were just the night sounds of the river. One last slide, and he was safe in the bushes. He grinned at Tim in triumph.

Silently they slipped away. 'Quiet as a snake,'

whispered Tim. A twig snapped somewhere along the bank. The GI turned. He saw the fish were gone. He leapt to his feet, drew his revolver, and stared fearfully out into the empty darkness.

'Fancy taking our fish,' breathed Tim, as they sprinted up to the bridge, 'when they have all that food of their own.'

'One each,' said Harry. 'Does Lillie like fish?'

'Thanks.' said Tim. 'Dad never did have a clue about keeping her fed.'

Chapter Thirty

Mackerel and cod were laid out on the fish stall in the market square. On the rotten apple man's stall were orange carrots, white cabbage, pale turnips with purple tops, glossy green leaves, crisp celery. Open sacks of earthy potatoes leaned heavily at the side. Harry could almost taste the soup his mother used to make.

He sneaked a small potato into his pocket and glanced furtively round. The queue on the other side of the barrow had the mean old greengrocer's full attention. He reached out again. Two, bigger this time. He slipped them into his other pocket. The greengrocer still hadn't noticed. Serve him right for the rotten apple trick.

A grab on his collar made Harry freeze. Then he recognised the pull. He curled round out of the grip and grinned. 'Hi, GI!'

'What's in your pockets?' said Mike sternly.

The greengrocer spun round. Harry frowned. Surely Mike understood.

'Holes!' he said, inventively. He pulled one pocket out to demonstrate, hiding the one potato in his hand as he did so. There was a hole, a small one, but Mike wasn't fooled. He held out his hand.

Harry winked at him. Mike ignored it. Harry pulled away angrily.

'C'mon,' insisted Mike, in no mood to argue. 'What's in your hand?'

'Never trust a GI.'

'Never!'

Reluctantly Harry passed over the potato.

'Hey!' called the greengrocer indignantly.

'And the rest.'

Harry pulled the two potatoes from his other pocket, anger and fear welling up inside him. The greengrocer loomed over him, glowering. How long did you get in prison for stealing potatoes? His mum had been thrilled with the fish, thinking he'd caught it, but this? She'd kill him! And if Lewis heard, it would be yet another opportunity to get clouted.

'How much?' Mike asked.

The greengrocer was quick to reply. 'A tanner. Each!'

'Sixpence?'

'Each,' said the greengrocer firmly.

Mike gave him a withering look but paid up. He held the potatoes out expecting a paper bag for that price. 'Bought and paid for,' he said.

'Right?'

The greengrocer nodded. Accepting them back, agreed and packaged, Mike walked off with them, leaving the greengrocer narrowing his mean little eyes. 'You're not even local, you!'

Harry backed away fast and chased after Mike. 'Hey!' he cried, breathlessly, trying to keep up with the GI's determined stride.

Mike turned on him. 'I can't believe you did that! Don't you know stealing is wrong? Don't they teach you that in school?'

'We can't grow stuff anymore. It was for my mum.'

'She tells you to do that?' Mike glared at him. 'Your mom?'

Harry hung his head. 'No.'

'No. Right!'

'You Yanks have loads of food and money,' Harry said accusingly. 'You don't what it's like.'

'And the British are the most law abiding nation in the world,' said Mike, 'with the best justice system, Harry. They're decent, fair and honest. That's what it says in my manual. Honest!'

'I got a job in the mornings!' he countered. 'Milk round.'

'So pay for what you want!'

He wished he didn't care what Mike thought. 'I'm going be a soldier one day. Like you.'

'You want war? Better being some safe stay-at-home guy, believe me. Land. Relationships. Family. Stuff like that.' He was still cross. 'Build a house. Didn't you tell me your dad did that?' He was walking again, but maybe not so fast. Glancing at his watch, he headed across to the station steps, and sat down in a patch of bright sunlight. Harry sat down next to him. For a few moments they didn't speak.

'I miss the beach.'

'Where I was raised there's no beach. No green fields and hedges. Just wide fertile golden country. In a good corn year the combine harvesters just roll.' Mike gazed back along the old narrow street. 'It was tough leaving my home to come and fight your war.'

Harry thought about it. 'Are you afraid in case you die?'

'When I see my first real bullet coming at me, I sure as hell will be!'

'My dad is never afraid!'

'No?' Mike sighed. 'Okay. Well, afraid can be useful. It's somewhere for brave to begin.'

More silence.

'I wish I had the photograph.'

'What photograph?'

'Of my dad. It was left behind. Mum left it behind.'

'Forgotten, huh?'

'No! Well, maybe. I think it's because she's taken up with Lewis. It was him. He wouldn't let us go back for it.'

'Who's Lewis? A GI?'

'Much worse! He's that ugly Warden.'

Mike grinned. 'Somebody's worse than us GIs then!'

'GIs aren't so bad.'

Mike laughed right out loud. 'Sure.'

'Lewis is really horrible. Picks on me every chance. I hate him.' He reached down for a small stone. 'He wants Mum to himself. He tells her what to do and he's always complaining about Peppy and me. Saying we do things when we don't.'

'Peppy's your kid sister?'

He nodded. 'Penelope.'

'And your mom likes this guy?'

Harry frowned, thinking hard about it, not sure how to explain. 'I think she's sort of afraid of being on her own,' he said, 'and Lewis knows it.'

Silence again.

'So a milk round, huh?'

'Milk to drink, and one and sixpence a week.'

'I'm impressed.' Mike got to his feet. 'See anything of that big guy?'

Harry pulled a face. 'Same school.'

They walked up the station steps.

'You're taller.'

'How come you're here?' Harry asked, feeling taller.

'I'm on leave,' said Mike. 'The last for a while. Then we're off.'

'Where?' But they were inside the station and the train was chug-chugging in.

'Still no letter,' Harry said, through the rush of steam. Mike glanced at him and frowned. 'From my dad.' The train shunted and squealed to a halt.

Mike nodded. 'Missing. You said.' He gazed past him for a moment. 'You know,' he said, looking directly at him again, 'you're like having a kid brother, reminding me I should write to my mom.' He got out a pencil and a scrap of paper. He wrote something and tucked the paper down into Harry's jacket pocket. 'My address. For one day when this old war is done.'

'Okay.'

Mike grinned. 'Hey, I was up early looking for curlews on the Ley last week.' He handed him the bag of three potatoes. 'Take these home. And don't steal them next time.'

'Okay.'

Bursts of steam frilled along between the platform and the train. Doors opened and banged shut. The guard took out his whistle. People boarded.

'Don't let the Lewis guy get to you, huh?' Mike cuffed him affectionately. 'If I don't see you again...' Then, 'You take care, you hear?' For a brief moment, a hug full of warmth, a hug like hugs from the past.

Mike showed his papers to the guard. The whistle blew. He climbed on board, slammed the green door behind him, pushed the window down. The stationmaster raised his flag.

Harry swallowed, fighting back tears. His vision of Mike blurred...Mike waving... his father waving... always somebody leaving. The train pulled away, chugging off down the line, its trail of white steam melting into the afternoon mist.

Chapter Thirty One

'How did she get out there?' Harry and Tim threw down their school bags. Lillie dangled perilously from the pulley beam above them.

'Bet she was trying to see over to the station. She hates Dad working away.'

Lillie stared down, whimpering with fright. Below Tim darted around trying to see whether her woolly scarf was caught as well as her sleeve. 'It could strangle her if she falls.'

Wriggling like a worm on a fishing line, Lilly reached out to catch hold of the splintered wood above her head and kicked her feet against the roof to get a footing. A slate dislodged, slid down and crashed on the ground beside them.

'There is the door, you know!' Harry cried, rattling the handle. 'Why would she climb out the roof hatch?'

'Dad locks her in. He gets into trouble from Lewis when she hangs around at the station.' Tim glanced urgently round the untidy yard. 'Anyway we couldn't reach her from inside. Not enough to pull her in.' He pointed to some old wooden crates. 'Any good?'

Above them there was a sharp ripping sound and a squeal from Lilly as she dropped a little. 'Quick!' Harry cried. They grabbed the crates.

'Don't move, Lillie!' he called, looking up and wincing at the thought of her falling. They stacked crates against the wall. Tim began to climb. The pile wobbled, and though Harry threw all his weight against it to steady it, that didn't make any difference. And if Tim or Lilly fell, the rough ground would be a very hard landing.

Balancing unsteadily at the top, Tim still couldn't reach her. 'Lillie, stretch your foot down.'

'No!' Harry cried. 'If you do catch her foot, and her sleeve gives way, you'll both fall.' He tried to think what else to do. 'Any straw, anywhere?'

'Stay there, Lillie,' said Tim, trying to calm her. He climbed down, which was worse than climbing up. It was obvious bringing Lillie down like that wouldn't work anyway. 'Straw?'

'We could make something to fall on and then unhook her,' said Harry. 'Or at least we'd have a chance to go for help.'

Lillie began to cry.

'Mattress!' said Tim.

They put their shoulders to the locked door. It was surprisingly strong. Harry tried his penknife.

The sharp point drove through, weakening the wood round the lock with no trouble. A really hard shove and they were in. The one room with a hayloft Jed lived in with his two kids was rough and untidy. It was a roof over their heads but there was little point locking it up.

Lillie screamed. There was no time to lose.

'What if she hadn't got hooked when she slipped?' cried Tim, as they dragged Jed's old mattress out into the yard and positioned it. 'It's all right, Lillie,' he called. 'If you fall, you'll end up on our dad's bed now.' Lillie shook her head, terrified.

'I'm going up,' he said to Harry. 'Give me the penknife.'

'My penknife? Why?'

'I'll cut her free.'

Harry passed it over.

'And you have to catch her.'

Harry caught his breath. Catch her? How could he possibly catch her?

A minute later Tim leaned out through the hatch. 'Ready?'

Harry stood on the mattress and took a deep uncertain breath and watched Tim half climb out, holding on with one unsteady hand and reaching down with the other towards the splintered wood that hooked her. 'At least it's not caught her scarf,' he called. All the same he tried to encourage her to take the scarf off. She clung to it with her free hand, her eyes wide, as if it was all that was keeping her together. Eventually Tim convinced her to unwind it. She held it out, swinging slightly as she let it go. Harry watched it slide slowly and silently down the grey slates towards him. He caught it easily, but catching her woolly scarf was not catching her.

Up on the roof Tim reached further out, stretching as far as he dared. He could just reach Lillie's shoulder. He had the penknife out now. The blade glinted. 'Ready?'

Harry stared up in utter dread, shaking. Would he ever be ready? Lillie was so little, so breakable. She might die falling. She might die landing. He looked at her scared face and the size of her and the way she dangled there. He had to be ready. Tim was cutting through what was left of her sleeve. She started to scream. Inside his head Harry began to scream himself.

'What are you doing?'

He turned to see Lewis striding towards him. He looked back to see Tim's frightened face and Lillie sliding down the roof towards him.

'What the hell are you doing?' Lewis's words

were ringing in his ear, but Lillie's screaming was louder, and far, far more urgent. He held out his arms, focussed on her, only her, as if time was standing still. She was floating down, flying slow motion towards him. He snatched in his breath and held his arms out wider, and stepped forward under her, quite sure he would die, and she would too. She hit him straight on the chest, and they fell together onto the mattress with a dull thud.

He gasped for breath. He tried moving, expecting to feel broken somewhere, but everything worked. He gasped again. This time his lungs filled. But Lillie wasn't moving.

'Lillie?' he whispered, dreading what might have happened.

Lillie's breathing started suddenly in short sobbing puffs. Her face was warm against his, and her little sparrow weight began moving against his body. All of her. Nothing limp or broken. She was winded, but they were both still alive. 'You're safe, Lillie,' he whispered. 'You're all right.' He put his arms around her and laughed that they had done it.

'What's going on? What's that child up to?' Lewis leaned over Harry, his shadow dark and his baggy boiler suit uniform huge, threatening.

Lillie clung on to Harry and began to cry. 'Get off! You're frightening her!'

Tim swung out of the door. 'Lillie!' he cried, pushing Lewis out of the way and gathering her up.

'What was the child doing on the roof?' roared Lewis. 'Her father will hear about this! I've told him and told him. If he can't stop her antics, I'll make sure she's taken into care.'

'You leave her alone!' cried Tim, shielding her.

Lewis turned on him. 'You too, boy! You'll be gone too, soon as look at you!'

Harry jumped up and pulled Lewis round. 'It was my fault,' he said. 'I dared her. She climbed out on the roof because of me.'

Lewis shook him off and struck him hard. 'You irresponsible young lout! Mark my words, your mother will hear of this!'

'How dare you put a young child in danger?' Celia shouted at him when she heard. 'I'm not surprised Lewis hit you! What would your father have thought?'

Actually, Harry thought, examining the bruise coming up on his shoulder, Dad might have rescued Lillie the same way. How he hated Lewis for twisting the truth.

'They'll take you away, Harry. Lewis says they will put you in care.'

'But it wasn't like that, Mum!'

His mother began to cry. 'Lewis is the only person I can rely on.' She wouldn't listen to his account of the story. Since she'd known Lewis, she didn't seem able to believe anyone else.

Chapter Thirty Two

Tim was in rebellious mood. 'School? Why go to school?'

'We're supposed to.'

'Can't leave Lillie alone all day long, can I?' He swung idly round a lamp post.

'Isn't she all right with the WVS today?'

'While Lewis's jeep is up by the Town Hall, she is.' He pulled away from the post and jumped in a gutter puddle. 'How come he gets a GI jeep?'

Harry shrugged. 'Maybe he's working for them now.'

'Well, he can't be the Warden here. There must be one already.'

'He's still in the uniform. There'd be more than one. Everyone has to do something. It's a big place.'

Tim grimaced. 'He was so nasty to everyone back home. It would've been good if he had lost his job!'

'Not if he got a better one with the Yanks.'

'You're right,' said Tim, disappointed. 'Let's go up to the square.'

Several US officers were in conversation on the

steps. The Town Hall was their headquarters now. There was no sign of Lewis but his jeep was parked right outside the entrance.

'How do you know it's his?'

'I know,' said Tim.

Several yards in front of it, was an official looking black car.

The officers on the steps went inside. There was no one else in the street. 'Come on,' whispered Tim. They crossed the road to the jeep. Tim climbed into the driving seat.

'Be careful,' Harry giggled. 'What if he catches us?'

'He won't.' Tim turned the steering wheel back and forth, and pumped the pedals up and down.

'Someone will see us.'

Tim gave him a withering look. 'You're scared!' He lent over the back and yanked a rug aside. Underneath were boxes marked US Army. Bottles of Scotch Whisky. Packets and packets of cigarettes. He gave out a long low whistle. 'What's that worth?'

'Quick!' Harry urged. The Town Hall door was opening. 'Quick! Someone's coming.'

Tim leapt out, then reached back in.

'Quick!'

They darted over the road and hid in a

doorway.

'That's somebody pretty important,' Harry whispered, as two GIs followed a senior officer down the hill past Lewis's jeep towards the polished black car. One of the GIs opened the car door and saluted.

'Maybe he's a General,' Tim whispered.

Another officer came out the Town Hall door. 'Sir?' The General looked back. The officer paused by Lewis's jeep. He put his foot up on the riding board to balance his small attaché case on his knee to open it.

Tim nudged Harry and grinned.

'What?'

Lewis's jeep moved suddenly, began to roll. The officer lost his footing with a shout. The open case fell away from him, scattering the contents. The other men spun round, leaping after the flying papers in panic. The General and the GI jumped back as the jeep shunted into the official car with a heavy crunch.

'Who's is that?' thundered the General.

Lewis, emerging from the Town Hall door, stared in confusion at the officers chasing papers and the red faced General assessing the damage to both vehicles. One of them lifted the rug. 'What's all this?'

'Cramer?' roared one of the others.

Tim darted away. Lewis looked across and for one split second his eyes met Harry's. Harry turned and ran for his life.

'What did you do that for?' Harry demanded, as they strolled along the riverbank.

'Anyone can leave a handbrake off,' said Tim, 'He can't prove anything.'

'He saw me,' said Harry.

'What can he do? He can't say there were kids in the jeep. That's US property. And all that stuff he had in the back? That's worse.'

'He'll remember.'

'Good though, wasn't it?' said Tim, grinning. 'And he might not be so popular with the Yanks now.'

Chapter Thirty Three

The old grey carthorse whinnied as the milk cart rolled along, its wheels bumping and squeaking, crying out for oil. Three of the big churns were already empty. In the last, creamy white milk dimpled and swirled to the rhythm of clip-clop hooves on rough cobbles.

The dawn air was damp and sweet with the scent of spring, and a hint of rain on the way. But Harry knew Ernie the milkman couldn't smell any of that. Red-nosed, and snuffling loudly into his large white handkerchief, he seemed content to lead the old horse along, and let Harry do all the legwork. Harry didn't mind. It was fun working on his own, as if the round was his, knocking at the door of every house, with none of Ernie's silly old chat. He collected the jugs, filled them up, and delivered them straight back. He took the money and sometimes got to keep the penny change.

This was the last street on the round, steps up to each door, a terrace of grand houses. Normally he was packed off before this. Ernie did these calls himself, but today he was too sick to bother.

He ran up the steps and knocked at the door. It opened and Mrs Prouse stood there in her dressing gown. 'Harry!' she said, as surprised as he was.

'Well!' She dropped her money into her jug and passed it to him. He scooted back to the cart, hoping if he was quick enough she wouldn't have time to call Frank out. But it was early. Frank was dangerous, but he was lazy. Almost certainly he was still in bed.

Harry dipped the jug deep into the metal churn. Fresh white milk streamed over its edge as it came up. But suddenly he stared at it in horror. He'd forgotten the money inside. Now what? If he poured the milk back into the churn, the coin might slip in with it, unreachable till later when the churn was washed out. At the end of the round the shilling would certainly be missed.

Up ahead Ernie was blowing his nose. Harry swung round to check if Mrs Prouse was watching. She had her back to him, looking into her own hall. Calling Frank? No time to worry about Frank.

Using the side of the cart for cover, he reached his grubby hand down through the creamy liquid. Scrabbling on the bottom, he captured the silver shilling and brought it to the surface. He smeared it across his sleeve and threw it into Ernie's box. He wiped his hands on the putrid old cart rag, took Mrs Prouse's penny change and the full milk jug, and headed back up her steps. Thankfully there was no sign of Frank, but as he waited for her to turn round, he saw to his horror a dark swirl on the creamy white surface. Any second now Mrs Prouse would see it and cause trouble. He held his breath as she swivelled round.

Unexpectedly she stepped past him. 'Ernie?' she called to the milkman. 'You all right?'

Harry took his chance. He sloshed his finger quickly around in the milk. The dark swirl mixed in and disappeared.

From beyond the horse, Ernie abandoned his streaming nose and waved his hanky weakly. 'Influenza,' he croaked.

'Good boy,' said Mrs Prouse, turning back to Harry and taking the jug. 'Doing his work. Don't want any nasty germs, do we? I wish my Frank would get himself started like you.' Harry held out her penny. 'Keep the change,' she said, and closed the door.

Jubilant, Harry pocketed the penny and skipped lightly up the steps next door to ring the bell. No answer. He rang it again. A young woman, his mother's sort of age, opened the door. Her eyes were red and tearful. She stared at him vacantly.

'Milk, Mrs?'

She frowned, confused.

'Milk?' he repeated.

She shook her head and dug into her dressing gown pocket. 'He's dead, see?' she said, thrusting a telegram into Harry's hands. 'There's no money for milk now...' He looked at it. *It is my sad duty to inform you...*

'He never wrote to me. Never said where he was.'

The words on the telegram seemed to lose their places and move around. Only the last ones were still as still. ...*missing, presumed dead.*

Harry pushed the telegram back at her and retreated down the steps, shocked. He imagined Mrs Latcham calling up the stairs to his mother, 'There's a telegram for you.' Or Lewis bringing the news. Or worse, much worse, how did Mum know Dad was missing? Had there already been a telegram like that? Suddenly he didn't want to be doing milk. He gulped down his cup of it. The last calls Ernie could do himself, germs or no germs. And he told him so. 'What's up?' Ernie shouted after him.

Chapter Thirty Four

It was raining. In the grim schoolroom Harry's head was full of tears and telegrams … *Missing, presumed dead.* But if he asked he might find out…

He heard Tim hiss at him from along the row.

'What!'

Miss Rosewall was helping one of the little seven year olds to catch up. School here was such a stupid mix of ages. The kids in his own row fiddled with their pencils and stared out the window. One was folding paper to make an aeroplane. Frank's brother Bill, skinny and a bit slow, probably from being beaten up by Frank all the time, was asking why he had to sit with these silly little kids at the front when he was nine. 'Why is Lillie sitting back with Tim?'

'Yeah,' called Frank from the back. 'And she's not even six, dumb bell.' Lillie slid down in her seat, and looked even smaller. Bill went red.

'Silence!' boomed Miss Rosewall.

Harry glanced back. The eldest in the class, and the only reason Frank bothered to turn up to lessons, was fourteen-year-old Margaret. Magnetic Margaret. Clever and pretty. They were meant to be sensible, the ones in the back row, but she spent most of her time passing notes to Frank and two other older boys, and there was always a low buzz at the back, evidence of something going on.

Harry was glad he wasn't there. And not just because of Frank. Margaret's gaze always made him feel anxious, and untidy. No one here was well dressed, but with un-darned holes in his jumper and socks, and cardboard inside his shoes, he was the worst. Frayed at the edges and outstandingly scruffy.

'Clearly,' Margaret had announced in the schoolyard, 'your mother doesn't care.'

'This country was invaded,' said Miss Rosewall, pointing to a long picture pinned across the black board, 'by a foreign force in ten sixty-six. Who were these invaders?'

Harry fiddled with his shoe, and the shreds of wet cardboard sticking out of the hole in the bottom of it. The shoes were bad enough, but the cardboard was giving up now. He tried stuffing it back thinking if he said… if he said, Mum, how do you know about daddy? Was there a telegram…

'What are you doing?' whispered Gwen, the paper-thin ten year old who always managed to end up sitting next to him.

'Nothing.'

Ronnie, next to Gwen, leaned over to see what she was looking at. Harry cast them both a filthy look and turned his attention back to his shoe.

'Well?' asked Miss Rosewall, waiting for some kind of response.

Margaret came to the rescue. 'The Normans, Miss. Big – strong – Normans!' The boys near her giggled, and shifted noisily in their seats. Frank, with his eyes fixed on her, began to rock his chair back and forth.

Harry ignored Gwen's shy giggle, and focussed again on his shoe, wondering if talk about newer shoes might be carefully turned round to telegrams.

'All right. Calm down,' said Miss Rosewall. 'And this wonderful Bayeux tapestry...' There was a definite lack of attention in the middle of the room. 'Gwen?' she snapped.

Gwen looked round. 'Yes, Miss?' she stammered.

'So, what does this tapestry show, Gwen?' Gwen went red and shrivelled down into her seat. 'Ronnie?' Ronnie shrugged and shifted closer and supportively towards Gwen. He shot an accusing glance at Harry.

Harry poked his finger into the gap in his shoe between the sole and the upper and wondered if second hand was possible, or market ones, maybe. He might just have enough saved.

Miss Rosewall narrowed her eyes, sizing up the problem. 'All right, Ronnie. Tell everyone, will you? What is so interesting about Harry?'

Harry looked up. Tim had his warning face on. Lilly was kneeling up on her seat. Miss Rosewall was coming.

'It's his shoe, Miss,' said Ronnie, quick to shift the blame.

'Harry?' She was beside him now, pulling him to his feet. 'Show me!' she said, smacking her hand on his desk. He put his foot up. The cardboard, shredded before and fiddled with once too often, fell out in tufts. Everyone stood up to see. Margaret giggled. Frank laughed loudly. Even Tim was grinning, and lifting Lillie up so she could see!

'It's very untidy coming to school like that, Harry Beere. This is Totnes, not the sticks. And is that the very best cardboard your mother could find?' Everyone shouted with laughter, and began to chant, 'Cardboard, cardboard.' Miss Rosewall seemed pleased. She had them again, and with her joke, not theirs. 'Silence!' she commanded, waving Harry's foot off the desk. 'Well then, Harry Beere, what was I saying?'

He looked at her blankly.

Everyone tittered. 'I was asking what does the Bayeux tapestry show?'

'I don't know, Miss.'

'There's a war on, Harry Beere! Our men are away fighting for us! Men full of duty and honour.' She picked on one of the holes in his old jumper, hooked her finger into it and propelled him along the aisle towards the black board. She planted him in front of the picture. 'The Bayeux tapestry shows the Norman army from France landing on the British coast. The Normans had horses and arrows, and their leader, William the Conqueror. Invasion!' She stabbed her index finger at the main action. 'And there! There is King Harold's defence of the realm.'

He stared at the picture, at the invaders, riding, rushing forth with arrows and spears towards the King's defending forces. Invasion! He could hear shouting, the hooves of the horses, the clash of steel swords.

'Your father's away fighting, isn't he?' Miss Rosewall's voice called from somewhere far away. Her words began to spin around in his head. An arrow pierced King Harold's eye, the power of its thrust forcing the king back off his horse. A man full of duty and honour dying to defend his country.

Chapter Thirty Five

'So, milk boy.' Frank stood baring his way. 'Your mother still seeing the Warden?'

Harry kept his eyes down, feeling a red rush of fury rising up his neck.

Frank poked fiercely at the hole in his jumper Miss Rosewall had found. 'No time for mending your clothes, that's obvious.'

Last out of the schoolroom, Harry knew he was on his own. The only good thing was Frank was on his own too. He gripped his jacket pockets tightly, frustrated at how powerless and afraid he could feel.

'Saw her leaving on the train this morning.'

He raised his gaze warily. 'What?'

Frank laughed triumphantly. 'You don't know!'

Harry began to shake inside. He longed to get past and out into the schoolyard. 'What do you mean?' His voice choked in his throat.

'Your dad know what she's up to?' sneered Frank.

Harry's pulse snapped. 'She's not up to anything!' he shouted and shoved Frank hard.

Frank fell back against the wall and slid down it. Harry leapt over him and burst out the door. The yard was slippery and wet from the earlier rain. Quick! Who were enemies and allies in a stand up fight? Margaret leaning provocatively against the wall? Her sudden smile was worrying. Skinny Bill, hands in pockets. Too fearful. Over by the fence Ronnie was showing Tim with his own shoe how Harry's had fallen apart. Disloyally Tim was enjoying the joke. Two of the other older boys, more likely to help Frank, blocked the main gate. There were the little kids, and Lillie. All far too small to call on. But more importantly... saw Mum leaving? He glanced back. Frank was up and lumbering out towards him, glowering, spoiling for a punch up. The side gate? The lane leading down towards the market? He nipped round the corner and ran.

Breathless, his feet freezing and blistered by soggy cardboard, Harry let himself in. Mrs Latcham's coat wasn't on the hook. The house was worryingly silent. He took the stairs two at a time and flung open the bedroom door.

Seeing his mother sitting there filled him with so much relief he could cry. When she turned, she looked frightened. 'It's all right, she'll be fine.'

His relief vanished. 'Who'll be fine?'

'Peppy. She'll be fine. They take children to live away from the bombs.'

'Bombs?'

'Peppy.'

'What? No bombs fall here! Mum?'

'She went on the first train.'

'What first train? Where? Who's looking after her?'

'I want her to be safe.'

'Where's she gone?'

'She'll be safer, Harry.'

'Who says?' But he knew exactly who.

'Lewis advised me. He's taken care of everything.'

Harry grabbed her trembling hands trying to shake Lewis out of her. 'Peppy gets frightened and cries when she's scared. How can you let him send her away on some train? She needs you, Mum! She needs me! She's only little. One day we'll go home to the beach and…'

There were tears in her eyes. 'I'm trying to do the right thing, Harry. I need her to be safe. There might be an invasion. Bombs fall. And I'll have more time now. I can work. Lewis says it's for the best.' She glanced nervously past him.

'Why do you listen to him? I'll help you. I'll

210

work. I'll do anything. Where's Peppy gone? Where is she?'

'I don't know. Lewis says it's better if only he knows.'

'What?' He threw her hands off and stared at her in horror. She looked really frightened. A shadow moved across the connecting door.

Lewis stood there, framed. 'How dare you send my little sister away!' He turned on his mother again. 'Why did you let him?'

'It's high time,' Lewis thundered, 'you showed some respect for your mother.'

'Can't you see how horrible he is? What about Dad?'

'Don't be rude, Harry.'

'Rude? Rude? My dad's missing and now my little sister is!'

'We'll talk later. Lewis is going back to Slapton tonight.'

'Shut up, Celia.'

'The photo!' Harry cried. 'He could get it for you.'

Lewis was unbuckling his belt. 'We should get a few things sorted out here and now.'

'Tell him, Mum! Dad's photo. It's back there! It's in my box.'

Lewis's eyes fixed on him. The belt snaked

through its loops. 'Your mother doesn't want some stupid photo.'

Harry ran at him.

Celia tried to leap between them but Lewis pushed her onto the bed out of his way. Harry caught him though, full force. Lewis fell hard to the floor. He grabbed Harry roughly by the arm and swung him down too. 'I'll have you, boy! You wait! Attacking a Duty Warden! You'll be locked up before you know it.'

Celia screamed and wrenched Harry up and away, and though he struggled, and kicked and punched the air, she held him back with an iron grip.

Lewis jumped to his feet glowering at her. 'You choose!' He grabbed his belt and lurched threateningly at Harry as he stormed out. The front door downstairs slammed behind him.

Celia's hands loosened. Harry could feel she was crying. He shook her off and backed away accusingly.

'Lewis says he'll marry me,' she sobbed. 'You children need a father. What else can I do? We need some kind of home.'

Harry stared at her in utter disbelief. 'Why do you always do what he says?'

She looked at him defiantly. 'How do you

think we'd have managed if Lewis hadn't looked after us with food and paid the rent?'

'What about Daddy?'

'If Daddy loved me, if he was alive, he'd write! There's been nothing. No letters, no word to me for months. What am I supposed to do? He's dead, Harry. Gone.'

'He thinks we're in Torcross,' shouted Harry. 'You never filled in the forms. What if he comes home? He'll never find us.'

'He won't come home! It's a new life for us now. Forget all about that beach.'

'You don't care about Daddy.'

Celia lunged at him. Her slap stung his cheek and he fell back, stunned. Behind him, the shepherdess wobbled and fell. It hit the floor and smashed, and Celia cried out in fury. Harry ran blindly, out onto the landing and down the stairs. He heard her calling after him.

'Harry! Harry!'

Ahead of him the front door opened and Mrs Latcham stepped in. She looked up in astonishment at Celia shouting down the stairs, and him running towards her. She struck out angrily but he thrust her roughly aside and rushed out the door.

The mean greengrocer saw him coming, lurched out to grab him, but he skipped out and past him, and ran on across the square. The shouts behind him faded as he zig-zagged through the rows of stalls and queues. On the far side of the market, Tim and Lillie sorting through a charity box saw him swing round the corner towards the High street.

Under the shadow of the arched East Gate he glanced breathlessly over his shoulder. No one was chasing him, but people noticed his hurry. Some turned to watch him. He eased up into an urgent walk, headed on down to the river. It waited, a barrier of deep, dark, muddy water under murky rain clouds.

When he reached the bridge he crossed it without looking back. The air was cold, stinging his face as he reached the other side. He pulled his jacket closer, grateful for the old jumper underneath it, holes or not. He strode on up Bridgetown Hill, leaving behind Totnes and the squall of rain over it. Ahead of him the clouds parted and the sun trickled through, lighting up the last of the day.

The few houses and roads of Bridgetown thinned out. He chose the smaller lanes past high-banked hedges and patchwork fields. He was surprised blossom was already falling like flakes of pink snow. Daffodils and clumps of yellow primroses hugged the grass verges. A single blackbird sang as he passed. Beams of late afternoon sunlight striped across the landscape. He went on walking. Putting one foot in front of another was all that mattered.

Chapter Thirty Six

With trembling fingers Celia gathered up the pieces of the smashed shepherdess. Everything she had was breaking up.

At least they had a roof over their heads and food on the table. All the same she wished, wished, she hadn't let Lewis send Peppy away. But he was so sure trouble was coming, warning her how close the enemy was, that an invasion might only be a whisper away. Bombs had robbed her of all her family and that new doodle bug fell out of the sky without the slightest sound or warning. Every night now there were distant explosions down on the coast.

She twisted Harry's scarf round and round in her hands. She was on his side, of course she was, but he had to understand life wasn't the same anymore. He had to grow up.

A fox barked a warning somewhere. A bat skittered over Harry's head. He heard a scrape, perhaps a footstep, and for the first time since crossing the iron bridge over the river he surfaced from the monotony of marching. The air was chill but there was no wind. Over what looked like a creek, mist was drifting in pale layers and slowly rising up the hill ahead. Beyond that on the darkening horizon were flashes of light and distant rumbles, but it was not thunder. There were no clouds out there.

The thought of rain made him thirsty. He suddenly felt the sting of the blisters on his feet and the ache of tiredness in his legs. He stopped. For a moment the lack of movement made him dizzy. He reached out to an old oak tree to steady himself. Through a break in the hedge, lit by the rising moon, he saw a barn half hidden in the fold of the next hill. He squeezed through the hedge and tramped across the spongy red earth, longing for soft hay and a place to rest.

A familiar smell of warm fur hide and digested grass drifted on the air by the barn door. He could hear the friendly munching of a cow. He crept in. She stood in her stall, her wide white and honey coloured rump to him. He hesitated, afraid if she was there, someone else might be, and he had no wish to be discovered. It occurred to him his mother might mind that he was gone as well as Peppy, but he didn't care. He wasn't going back. Anyway she wanted Lewis. He wondered if he would ever, ever be able to

217

forgive her.

The cow's ears twitched. If she had heard him, that would be enough to bring anyone else out into the open. He waited a minute, listening, but no one appeared. He approached carefully, smelling her warmth. She shifted on her feet as he stroked her hide, inclining towards him, enjoying the kindness of contact. He relaxed a little and looked round the barn. Moonlight fell on old straps, a broken saddle, stale straw. He found a rusty old bucket and crouched down beside the cow. He leaned his forehead in against her rump. She turned her head and blinked her brown eyes at him in surprise. For a moment he sat still, while she contemplated him. Then she returned to her amiable chewing. Soon there was warm white foaming milk squirting into the bucket. He drank it greedily, milked more and drank that too. With the comfort of the milk, exhaustion overcame him. He found a pile of sweet hay in a corner and crumpled down into it. The pleasant sound of the cow's pulling and chewing lulled him quickly into deep sleep.

'Harry?' Celia's anxious call echoed round the dark market square. There was no answer. She had no idea where he usually spent his time. But it wasn't so very late. Maybe she was worrying unnecessarily. He would come home, defiant, as late as possible, and she could say how ashamed and sorry she was for hitting him, and they could sit down together and talk about adult life, about growing up, about making the best of things. She stopped, listened. But it was her own footsteps on the cobbles she'd heard. She looked back. Her shadow stretched out behind her. The square was empty and silent.

Near the East Gate, the smell of beer and convivial banter in the Old Dart Inn spiked a pang of hunger through her.

Fish! She hurried down to the river. The moon glistened on the deep black water. Very far off, a rumble. Explosions again. She picked her way along the muddy bank calling, but there was no sound except the gushing river flowing away from her towards the sea.

Chapter Thirty Seven

He opened his eyes. The hay round him was streaked with dawn light. Above him criss-cross old wooden beams. Shadows.

'Where were you going?'

He sat bolt upright.

'Take some keeping up with, you do.' Tim hoisted himself onto the straw bale. He dangled his legs carelessly over the side and grinned. 'So where?'

Harry didn't answer. He wasn't sure he knew.

'In those awful shoes, too!'

Harry jumped angrily to his feet and brushed the hay off his jacket.

Tim waved an old pair of shoes at him. 'Brought you replacements.' For a moment Harry didn't take them. 'Best me and Lillie could find.'

He accepted them reluctantly. They were old but far better than his. They actually had soles.

'Hope they fit,' said Tim enthusiastically. He produced a piece of thick brown cardboard from his pocket. 'But just in case.'

'Thanks.'

Tim grinned. He reached for the rusty old

bucket and passed that over too. It was full of fresh milk. He jerked his thumb at the cow. 'Someone will be here any minute for her, I reckon.'

Outside the sun's rays streamed across the landscape outlining the hedge, making diamonds of the morning dew. They sat in the lane for the shoe trying on. Heavy after his old pair and slightly big, but with the addition of some cardboard and his socks, they fitted reasonably snugly.

Harry strutted up and down in them, pleased. 'Thanks,' he said, meaning it.

'So what happened?' asked Tim.

'Nothing,' he said, digging his new heel into the ground. Then, 'Lewis happened.'

'What, he takes her out and that?'

'He's sent Peppy away.'

Tim gasped.

'Evacuated, Mum says, but she doesn't know where. Worse, he wants her to marry him!'

Tim gave a long low whistle. 'What will happen?' he asked.

Harry gazed out over the field. He nipped off a sharp bit of skin at the side of his fingernail. Suddenly he knew. 'I'm going back for my dad's picture,' he said.

Tim stared up at him. 'Going back? What, to Torcross?'

Harry nodded.

'But it's no go down there. US occupied. Government orders.'

'I don't care.' He kicked a stone and then another. There was nothing like the power of shoes with some sole to them.

'It's easily a day and a half's walk and there's road blocks and stuff, Harry. Military police, people say. You'll be arrested.'

'So?'

Tim laughed and jumped to his feet. He did a kind of tap dance, his eyes shining. 'Mind if I come along?'

Chapter Thirty Eight

The mud-covered wheels squealed on the ancient stone water-bridge as the old farm cart trundled over it. Through the straw that hid them, Harry saw a village sign for Blackawton Cross. The cart turned up the hill and rattled along the ridge.

A sudden stop and a bump-bump. Harry dared to peer out again and nudged Tim. 'Look!' The farmer stood at the crossroads a short distance away. He lit his pipe and stared out across the land.

'Bet he won't dare go any further west,' whispered Tim, 'and nor should we.'

'You scared?'

Tim shook his head.

Harry pointed to a ditch beside the road. Keeping low, they clambered off and rolled down into it.

The farm cart had not long wheeled off without them when a military police jeep hurtled past. 'Hey,' whispered Tim, 'they're after you already.'

'There's some kind of patrol over on that hill.'

Tim followed Harry's line of sight. 'What do

you want your dad's picture for anyway?'

'If there's no photo, Peppy's got nothing to remember. You said it's only what your dad tells you about your mum.'

Tim ducked back down. 'Do you think Lilly's all right?'

'You don't have to come.'

'It's a prohibit-tated area.'

'Prohibited.'

Tim nodded. 'I don't reckon we'll get far.' All the same he followed as Harry scuttled off across the field to the cover of the first hedge.

In the corridor the uniformed secretary looked at Celia suspiciously. 'Lewis Cramer?' She yanked Celia out of the way as two Army officers strode past. 'He isn't here.'

'But I need to see him.'

'I'm sure,' said the woman disapprovingly, 'but we're all extremely busy right now. Military personnel are not available.'

'He's a Senior Warden.'

'Everybody's very busy.'

'Look,' said Celia, 'my son has disappeared. He's been gone since yesterday afternoon. I've searched everywhere.'

'And what are we supposed to do about it?'

'I'm sure Mr Cramer would help me. I know he was going down to Slapton, but surely he must be back soon.'

The woman narrowed her eyes at her. She flipped the page of the notebook she was carrying. 'Name and address?'

Celia gave it eagerly.

'It's a prank,' said the secretary, dismissively. 'He'll turn up. You know what boys are.'

'It's not a prank!' Celia cried, frustrated again. 'Why won't you listen to me?'

'I am listening.'

'If it was your son…'

'I suggest you go to the police station.'

'I've been there.'

'Then go home and wait. There is a war on.'

'Yes! There is a war on,' cried Celia. 'And that's precisely why I need to know my son is safe!'

Chapter Thirty Nine

The two boys kept close to the hedges, rested in ditches. Tim had bread, and they ate it all, first stop. They hid as armed patrols passed by. When men halted only yards away leaning on their jeeps and smoking fat cigars, it made Harry and Tim giggle they weren't seen. Everyone said these Americans were young, first time abroad. They chatted about food and pretty girls and dances. Of winning the war in weeks and going home heroes.

'Doesn't say much for them,' said Tim, 'letting two boys march across the territory they're guarding.'

'Maybe they feel safe here. Allies and that. Maybe they don't think to watch out.'

His legs were aching but Harry was first to crawl to the top of the hill. The midday sun lit up Start Bay and he lifted his head to smell the familiar salt wind blowing in from the sea.

'Hey! Look at all that army stuff,' whispered Tim.

There was barbed wire and barricading along

most of the beach, military vehicles and tanks at the eastern end, and gun emplacements all along the dunes.

'We'll never get past all that.'

'Don't come!'

'I won't.'

Harry considered the possibilities. 'Down behind the Ley,' he said, pointing. 'We could go that way.'

'We won't get through!'

'We got here, didn't we?'

'Maybe that was fluke.'

'Well, I'm going down. For my dad.'

'Some old photograph won't make any difference.'

'It will!'

Tim shook his head. 'No, it won't,' he said. 'And Harry, I've been thinking.'

Harry glanced out to sea. 'Lilly.'

Tim shifted on his elbows and looked out to sea too. 'Yeh.'

'I know. You have to.'

'I mean, what if Lewis starts on her next? Dad's hopeless.'

'I'm fine. See? New shoes.'

'You want me to tell her?' suggested Tim. 'Your mum. Where you are?'

'No!'

'No?'

Harry looked over his shoulder, the way they'd come. 'It will be just as hard going back, you know.'

'I'm a whiz at not being caught, me!' Tim said, grinning. 'Hope you find the picture.'

'I'll find it.'

Tim pushed himself up onto to his knees ready to make a start. He looked back.

'You've got to see Lillie through,' Harry said.

Tim nodded.

Harry scanned the hill. 'Nothing coming.'

'I'll be off then.'

'Be careful.'

'Bye.'

'Bye,' Harry said, but it stuck in his throat and didn't come out. He watched Tim darting down the hill in the shadow of the hedge. Slide down the ridge. He waited, holding his breath, straining to see. Finally the tiny dot disappeared into the distance.

He was on his own. And the photograph wasn't just a photograph. It was Dad. If Mum saw it, she'd remember and she wouldn't feel so afraid. She'd stop seeing Lewis, and everything would be all right. They'd find Peppy and show her the photograph and Peppy could keep in her head what Dad looked like too.

He took a deep breath. Which way down to the back of the Ley?

Chapter Forty

Late afternoon. Not a single bird out on the water. Not one. The Ley was mirror still. Harry moved along in the scrub behind it. On the lane leading round to the village he would have to be careful, but in spite of all the military on the beach, there was no movement anywhere in Torcross, just eerie silence.

He sneaked along to the row of cottages. A layer of thick dust lay like a cloak over them. Old Mr Thorn's front door was holed and splintered. Worse, only the front wall was still standing. Behind that the walls were gone. Harry stared in disbelief. A strange angle of light made huge cracks in the glass windows look like spider webs. Through them he could see the old bomb shelter on the slope, but the terraced walls leading to it had collapsed. The prized garden had fallen in on itself.

The rose bush still clung on, a reminder of old Mr Thorn's thin whiskery cheeks, and beady black eyes watching the GIs arrive. In spite of one tiny pink bud, all the leaves were ripped and coated in grime.

At the crossroads the corner shop was a heap of bricks and glass. The red posting box in the post office wall was there, but one more brick falling from the huge hole beside it would bring everything down. The damage was dreadful to every house by the beach. Harry glanced round nervously. Had the invasion happened?

In the dreadful silence he was sure he heard voices. Miss Markham hurrying everyone along, busy-bodying her way through the days. 'There is a war on, you know.' Amy Wardle walking along the road singing her favourite hymns. His father's voice from the beach, sprinting along the sand, turning, teasing, jogging on again. Mum laughing, calling them both home.

Harry swung round and looked up the hill. She would be leaning out the window. 'Harry... Harreeeeee...'

BOOM!!

The explosion lifted him off the ground and sent him sprawling onto the gravel, without air to breathe. Then like a wild sea, waves of air rolled back over him. He gasped it in. For one brief moment he saw the familiar white cottage shape on the hill before another explosion ripped the air apart again. Another shell whistled in behind that. His mouth was full grit and the ground under him was shifting, leaving nothing to reach for, nothing to grab. He staggered to his feet and tried to run, deafened and dizzy with shock, ducking as another shell whizzed in and landed where he'd been seconds before.

'Harry!'

He swung round. Past the smoke and debris he could see... Another deafening explosion burst nearby. The figure faded into smoke.

The smoke cleared and the rush of relief it was someone he knew was unexpected – but Lewis? 'What are you doing, boy! It's a prohibited area! Come here!'

Harry hesitated, swaying on his feet. There was no way through the black smoke and craters. He took an uncertain step forward.

Lewis moved sideways, held out his arms. 'Come on then,' he called. There was something odd in the tone of his voice... He moved again, the other way. 'This way.'

Which way? Harry wavered, unsure. Lewis smiled. 'I'll have you locked up for this!' Arms outstretched, he moved again, seeming to bar the way on three sides.

Harry backed away. The weird whistling came again. Whizzing. Another shell exploded behind him. The ground there erupted into fragments.

Lewis shouted. And then there was only smoke and dust and rubble, no Lewis, no air, and the terrifying, deafening noise again. The whole open corner where he cowered was being blasted away. Lewis, protected by the beachfront ruins, appeared again. 'Got you!'

The earth was opening up round Harry and he knew, he knew, any moment now the small piece of firm ground left to him would be blown up too. Stay here? Run to Lewis? Flying dust and grit stung his eyes. Another blast cut his hearing out completely. Now everything was happening in half-dark, without sound. Flash! Earth and stones burst into the air, travelling silently up through it, pausing, falling back. And still Lewis stood there, his arms stretched out and wide, powerful, impassable. Every suspicion, fear and hate Harry felt about the man rose up. 'I'll have you, boy!' screamed a voice inside his head. There was no way back.

But there was one other chance. All the shells and blasts were coming in from it, but on the beach… underneath it. The smoke and dust gave him cover as he hurled himself towards the Cut, leaping over holes and past chasms. A second more and he would be under the line of fire. A low mortar whistled in over the beach and hit.

There was a blinding flare of bright white light and the Cut exploded into bits.

Chapter Forty One

Celia felt the evening wind blowing in from the coast and heard the explosions. Everyone in Totnes stared at the glowing horizon, heard the barrage, and gathered in the square, frightened. 'That's live ammunition.'

Celia caught her breath. 'The invasion?'

'Should we go inland?' asked another. 'Are we occupied?' But other people said, 'No, no. They say it's the Yanks. They're training.'

'Reckon they're blowing the place to bits, doing what the enemy can't!'

'But are we safe? What's happening?'

With mounting panic Celia hurried through the darkening streets. She asked everyone but nobody had noticed a kid hanging around. Besides, didn't they all do that these days? She found Miss Rosewall. Her only suggestion was better shoes might be in order.

'My Frank knows everything that goes on,' Mrs Prouse assured her, but neither she nor Frank had seen Harry in the last twenty-four hours. Apparently Frank was quite disappointed. She caught Celia's arm. 'Miss Markham was killed in the bombing the other night. She was staying with her sister in the east end of London.'

'Oh, no!'

Mrs Prouse shook her head. 'Something is definitely up here. Have you noticed there are no men around? No GIs. No wardens.' Maybe the last was a veiled dig at her, but it was true. There were no servicemen around at all.

In the square Jed's little daughter Lillie was sitting alone in the shadows.

'Lillie! 'Where's... um...it's Tim, isn't it? Your brother?'

Lillie didn't answer. She drew a large circle on the dusty doorstep beside her.

'What are you doing out so late?'

Lillie looked up defiantly.

Celia frowned. She couldn't remember ever seeing the child without her brother before. 'Is my Harry with Tim?' she asked urgently. Lillie didn't answer, but from the flicker of recognition that crossed the little girl's face, she knew it was the right question. She perched on the step with her, and put her arm round the frail little shoulder. 'Where, Lillie?' Lillie leaned in to her, liking the warmth. 'Where is Harry?'

'Running.'

'Harry?'

'Mmm.'

'Where? Where was he running?'

Lillie leaned forward and pointed out to the High Street.

'Through there?'

Lillie nodded. 'On the bridge.' She looked up at Celia with big round frightened eyes. 'Will Tim come back soon?'

Celia hoped she'd find the boys at Jed's, but no. Nor was Jed home, but Lillie seemed happy enough to wait on her father's doorstep. Poor Jed. From snug tied cottage to this leaking old farm shed. But both his children were with him. Already she hated not having Peppy around. She wished she'd never agreed to let her go. She left Lillie and hurried home, anxious to check if by any miracle Harry might be back.

Turning the corner she saw a shadowy figure ringing Mrs Latcham's bell. The door opened. Light fell on a dark uniform and helmet. She caught her breath and sprinted along the road.

'What's happened? Have you found him?'

'Mrs Beere?'

'That's her,' said Mrs Latcham. 'What's going on?'

'Thank you, madam,' said the policeman. 'My

business is with this lady.' Mrs Latcham gave him a cold, accusing stare and closed the door.

The policeman looked at Celia. The street felt dark and quiet.

'What?' Celia cried desperately. 'Where is he?'

'I believe you have been making enquiries?'

'Oh, God, tell me! Have you found him?'

'There is a war on, Mrs Beere. Careless words cost lives.'

'What? What careless words?'

'You have been to the army offices?'

'Looking for my son. Yes.'

'Why would he be there?'

'He wouldn't be there! I was asking for the senior Warden from Slapton, Lewis Cramer.'

'Precisely. Why were you asking about Slapton?'

'Look! Do you know where he is?'

'Cramer?'

'My son! My son Harry! I've been to the police station too, twice for goodness sake. You must know that!' She stared at the policeman. 'Listen!' she said, trying to stay calm. 'My boy Harry has been missing for over twelve hours. I thought Mr Cramer might be able to help me.'

'And why would that be?'

'He knows him.'

'You realise, Mrs Beere, there are far more important things concerning the Wardens and the Military Personnel than tearaway boys.'

'Why? Why!' It made her so angry, this dismissing of Harry's disappearance. But as she watched his reaction to her questioning him, and how he avoided answering, it frightened her, as if there was something hidden and secret, something under the surface.

'What's going on?' she demanded. 'What's happening?'

'You go inside, Mrs Beere,' said the policeman firmly. 'Best not make too many enquiries right now. The boy will come back when he's hungry enough.'

She ripped Harry's bedroom apart, furious no one would help her. There must be something here to show what he might do, where he might go. Clothes? He was wearing most of them. It wasn't as if this was planned. The argument made him leave. If Lillie was right and Tim was missing too, that was some comfort. The two boys together would be safer than Harry on his own. She wished she'd asked Lillie where Jed was working – if the child knew. Maybe the boys had gone to some farm somewhere to find him. But that didn't tally with what Lillie said.

She unfolded an old drawing of Peppy's from the back of the drawer, but drew back from the collection of shrapnel and a spent bullet underneath it, painfully reminded of some boy in London discovered holding an unexploded bomb… No, no, concentrate. Where else? What else? What exactly was she looking for anyway?

She pitched his mattress back. Chocolate bars! But that wasn't surprising. GIs were always giving candy to kids. She searched the room again. There was nothing else.

'Harry,' she cried out. Totally exhausted, she flung herself down on her own bed. Since coming here, she'd had no time to notice what Harry did. Lewis constantly told her to send him out. So did Mrs Latcham. And Harry was keen to go. Indoors he was sullen now, and silent. Everything was her fault, every time. He blamed her for his dad going off to fight. For no news. For no letters. For leaving the beach. And now for sending Peppy inland to safety, when keeping her children safe was all she wanted. Even before they'd left the coast, Harry had been uncooperative. How stupid though to leave all his precious things behind! All those old shells and silly crab things from the beach. All his treasures. All…

She sat up, filled with absolute certainty. Of course! Why on earth hadn't she thought of it? She leapt to her feet, struggled into her coat and tied a scarf round her hair. She gathered up all the chocolate bars, stuffed a packet of biscuits into her pocket with them, and pulled on warm gloves.

Outside in the street the late night air stung her cheeks. When a policeman on his beat approached, she hid in shadow until he was gone. Then she hurried down to the river and out onto the bridge.

Chapter Forty Two

The air was warmer and a thin sea mist masked the moon. The sand and shingle was cool and damp from the tide that had earlier washed over it. There was no sign of Lewis following and the firing from somewhere out in the bay had stopped. His hearing was mostly back. The blast had deafened him only briefly. But blood dripped from the gash on his arm. If he could get down to the water he could clean it, wash the sand off it. But from the dunes near him came wisps of strong cigar smoke, and voices echoed around the Ley. Lewis could be there.

Three big guns and other equipment jutted out menacingly, facing the sea. Beneath their sight line, very close in, where pale white shingle and dune sand met, lay a small under-the-radar path to safety.

He knew this beach so well, but tonight it made him tremble. There was one place to hide. If it was still there. If he could find it. He crawled on as silently as he could, using the old monastery tower as a landmark to guide him. He ducked low under the gun barrels. Quiet as a snake, quieter, halting, holding his breath when the voices stopped and left dangerous empty silences. He crawled on when the conversation resumed, afraid with every trickle of sand or shift of shingle someone might discover him.

He paused in line with the ruined hotel. The wide gap between these guns and the next ones might be where the landmines started. He could just make out the top of the old tower. He should be exactly in line with the hide. He glanced back along the beach and took his bearings that way. Yes, he was sure. But the only way to the hide was up towards the dune. Right now there were plenty of voices. He took a terrible chance and raised his head just above the ridge.

The soldiers spotted something, a small round shape, moving on the dunes. One of them lifted his rifle to his shoulder and aimed. 'Go on! Shoot!' The crack of the shot and a sharp squeal echoed across the Ley. The dark shape fell and there was a cheer and laughter and a wave of torchlight as someone down by the Ley picked the corpse up like a trophy. Blood gushed from the wound in its neck. 'Rabbit bloody stew again.'

The rabbit's death took no more than a few seconds but it was enough time to scuttle onto the ridge and slip down into the shelter of the hide.

As the cheers and laughter died away, Harry shifted the bushes over him back into place.

'That another one?'

A flash of torchlight and a bullet whizzed through the bushes above. He cowered under the rock.

'Put that light out!' The angry voice turned Harry ice cold. He held his breath. But it didn't sound like Lewis was looking for him. Instead he was shouting about every light in Britain being out, every night and all night, for four long years, and what did they know about the blitz and being bombed bloody time after time after time? But these GIs didn't like Lewis, it was obvious. He was only a warden here. What right, they asked, did he have to tell them how the US army should behave? After a while the voices moved away. Lewis's too.

In the new silence and the darkness Harry reached out to feel the initials gouged into the rock. HB. JHB. He sank down by the comfort of them, far too exhausted to keep awake.

Chapter Forty Three

It rumbled suddenly into his dream. Something loud and threatening and dangerous. Harry woke with a start, for a moment surprised to find darkness and soft dry sand around him, the familiar sound of waves swishing on the shore; dragging, draining out, splashing in again, and pebbles skittering around in the foam. It sounded like the sea breathing.

But whatever woke him wasn't the sea. Through the rock windows he saw nothing except pale, shifting shingle and silver light stretching into the milky moon bay. But far out, blurred by a delicate shroud of sea mist, a throbbing orange glow was spreading out along the dark horizon. Bright bursts of light suddenly illuminated the night sky followed by another low thudding sound.

Out in the bay were dark shapes, ships, and then as first light crept into the sky, flat wide boats were racing in, and now he could hear the thrumming-hum of their engines. Above him on the dunes, there was movement, muttering. Voices, then urgent warnings, louder. Shouts.

Barked orders. Whoever was in those boats, they were closing fast on the beach. The hum of them swelled, beat louder across the water. Then in a vast swirl of salt water, the first one rasped up onto the shingle. Its bow crashed down hard on the pebbles. Men in helmets swarmed off, bristling with back packs and rifles, splashing through the shallows, advancing like warring crabs, spreading up the beach.

Ack! Ack! Ack! Above him defensive firing. But the crab men kept coming, heading up the shingle, over the sand towards the dunes, running, shooting.

A burst of big gunfire shook the ground, shook the air, forcing Harry to his knees. Sand rattled down on him from above. Daring to look again, he saw firing into the sea front houses, into Mrs Gales's, lines of sparks zipping through the air. He heard more shooting overhead from the dunes. Another landing craft crashed in. More fighting men spilled out. More shells landed, shaking the rocks round him. The air rushed in, and sucked away as fast. Shingle pebbles fell down through the bushes like rain. There was blood on them.

On the shore now were dark piles like storm driven seaweed. More landing craft spilled out soldiers. Some dodged the gunfire, ran up the shingle, dived into craters for cover. Others fell before they cleared the shallows. More craft swirled in. Tanks rumbled off. Men waded ashore behind them.

Shingle and beach sand and flesh exploded up into the air. Harry held on to the rock. Men he'd seen running weren't there any more. The screaming was, and the roar of tanks, the smell of diesel. Through a blur of tears and sweat, he saw more bullet traces. From upright and running, the bullet thrusts held men a brief moment in mid air. Blood spattered and sprayed out, then they crumpled down into stillness. Like puppets cut from strings they fell, into heaps of dark bloodied uniforms. More men leapt over them, round them but others caught the firing and fell too.

There were roars on the dunes above him, gunfire, screaming. 'It's live amo,' they were yelling. 'They're our own men for God's sake!' 'Cease fire!' But the firing didn't stop, and there were more shouts, 'Go, go, go!'

A landing boat in the shallows burst into flames. Gunfire exploded through a tank in a flume of bright orange. The beach was a burning bonfire. Sparks stung Harry's cheeks as he stared out at the mayhem. He'd seen blood, but never like this. Whoever these invaders were, he didn't want them here. Through it all, the screams, the firing, and the dying, but suddenly, worse than anything else – a voice.

A voice of someone passing right over him, and down the dunes. A man waving and shouting at a unit of men splashing ashore, 'Go back, take cover!' Bullets whizzed by, missing him by inches. The soldiers he was running towards stopped, confused, registering his warning. They dived back to their vessel. A shell exploded just where they would have been running, a sharp burst of shingle and dark sand.

'Mike,' Harry screamed.

Mike swung round. For a split second everything seemed to stop, then...

Thud, thud. Blood spattered and sprayed out into the air, and just like the others, in that same strange, slow motion puppet way, Mike folded slowly down onto the shingle and lay absolutely still.

Inside the hide Harry sank to his knees with a howl of utter despair.

Chapter Forty Four

A blanket of smoke hung over the beach. Far off blurred shapes of men and vehicles moved away along the sands. In the shallows the reflection of the misted morning sun looked like an American silver dollar. All was silent except for seawater lapping back and forth and Harry's shoes crunching into the shingle. His shadow fell across the body, its US uniform stiff with seawater and blood.

He leaned in close. Suddenly the eyes snapped open, shocking, bloodshot, eyelashes stuck together with sand. The filthy, dirty face under the helmet screwed up in distress.

Harry flung himself down on the bloody chest. 'I thought you were dead, GI,' he whimpered.

Mike's hand was heavy as it stroked his hair. 'Where did you come from, Harry Beere?' His voice was weak, whistling inside him.

Harry sat up urgently and looked along the beach. 'They're throwing dead ones into trucks. Searching them. Going through their papers.' He locked his arms under Mike's shoulders and began to pull. 'It's not safe here. We have to go.'

He heaved and hauled, grunting with the effort. The shingle slid slowly away under Mike. It was worse hauling him up the slope and over the dune. Harry gasped for breath, stretching his strength to breaking point. Mike moaned as the bush brushed his face. Then he moaned louder, opened his mouth to scream. There was horror on his face as he dropped away down through the ground.

Harry clambered in and leaned over him anxiously. 'I didn't hurt you, did I?'

Mike swallowed hard, shook his head a little. His eyes were floating.

'They came last night,' Harry told him. 'Like the Norman invasion. They killed everyone.' He reached up and pulled the bush back over the entrance. When he looked back Mike's eyes were closed.

Chapter Forty Five

The horizon was brightening as the truck rattled across country. The old farmhand driving it glanced across at Celia. 'Tis close to limit 'ere,' he said. 'You sure?'

'A bit further on,' she urged, nervously scanning the landscape for a reasonable target.

'Firing out there, last night, there be,' he observed.

'I heard.' She tried to suppress the panic in her voice, and say something normal. 'Must be long hours for you, working the land.'

He nodded. 'Too old for fighting. Who you meeting?'

'There.' She pointed to an old barn rising into view on the hill ahead. 'There.'

He narrowed his eyes at her, but he drove on slowly until he was halfway up the hill. 'No further,' he said firmly. The engine rattled and settled into a low stationary purr. 'Don't want 'em thinking I'm invading their territory.' He nodded towards the barn. 'Empty, that be.'

'Yes.' She climbed down, trying to smile as coyly as she could. 'You know what it's like.'

He sighed as if he wished it was him she was meeting. He pointed to a stile. 'You can cut up cross field.'

'Thanks,' she said. 'Thanks.'

Maybe he didn't believe she was meeting someone, but he had saved her several miles walk. She felt his eyes on her and heard the engine idling behind her as she climbed the stile. To convince him she waved towards the barn as if there really was someone waiting for her. She glanced back. Seemingly satisfied, he jerked the truck forward. She watched it turn around and go back the way it had come. When it was gone she strode past the barn and on over the fields.

Chapter Forty Six

Silence, except for the haunting cries of seagulls wheeling over the beach. Harry raised his head up through the bushes to eye level. A haze of smoke still hung in layers on the air, as if somewhere a huge fire was smouldering. There were sudden drifts of a tarnished, scraped metal sort of smell, but mostly just the stench of smoke and diesel. The sun stabbed beams of gold across the bay.

Below him a cough. Harry dropped down. Mike opened his eyes and shifted his leg painfully. 'Where am I?' he asked. Beads of sweat glistened on his forehead.

'My beach.' Harry crouched beside him. 'Was last night the invasion?'

Mike put his hand to his thigh. It came back up covered in blood.

Cutting the gashed uniform with his penknife revealed a bullet-wound, ragged, deep and bloody. Harry drew back, swallowing hard. 'You going to die?' he asked. Mike winced with pain and closed his eyes again.

Harry pulled off his jumper to get at his

grubby vest. The threadbare cotton ripped easily into strips. 'The Normans had horses and arrows,' he said, 'when they invaded.' He knotted three strips of vest together to make a tourniquet. It was a struggle with the dead weight of the leg and the confined space, but he managed to tie it tight round Mike's thigh. But he couldn't see how he could do that with the shoulder. What was needed was water to clean both wounds, like Tim had cleaned the gash on his leg with river water. But it was hopeless and far too dangerous to get Mike down to the sea.

He shivered and pulled his jumper back on. He checked the tourniquet, and gently brushed some of the caked sand off Mike's face. The helmet gave him an idea. 'Got to have this!' he said, removing it with difficulty. Mike was too far gone to notice.

Harry manoeuvred himself past Mike to the peephole. Down by the water's edge were two landing crafts. They cast long angled shadows across the shingle but there was nothing moving down there. Nothing moving anywhere. Just smoke drifting.

He edged the bushes back and raised his head and shoulders gingerly through the surface of the dune. Now he could see the source of the smoke, a crippled tank, all burnt out. At the far end of the Sands he could make out trucks, and men massing, but they were much nearer to Slapton village than Torcross.

He pushed the helmet out ahead of him, hauled himself up and out, and slithered down the bloodstained dune sand. With a quick check on the distant troops, he ducked down onto the beach. He crawled past craters in the shingle and crumpled heaps of uniforms that were dead men. There were tracks in the sand where other bodies had been dragged away. Now invasion had come to it, the beach, his beach, was a frightening place.

The smoke and this closest landing craft would give him cover, but if anyone was near, someone he couldn't see, the crunch of the shingle under his knees would certainly give him away. He crawled on, praying it wouldn't. A gull perching on the landing craft shrieked. With red-rimmed suspicious eyes, and wings thick with oil slick, it watched him steal along in the shadow of the hulk to the water's edge.

He crouched down low, eagerly breathing in the fresh salty air at water level. He sank his arms into the cold sea water, let it wash back and forth over his skin, suck away the blood and grime and fear. Each wave surge refreshed him. He cupped his hands and splashed his face, thinking of hot carefree summer days past, chasing his father, laughing, swimming in cool clean seawater.

The shingle dragged and rattled the helmet beside him. He filled it like a basin. The strips of his vest from his pocket he dipped into the waves to wash clean. The gull flapped its oily wings and rose fretfully up into the air and landed heavily again. Harry looked back, afraid. On the beach behind him everything was as quiet as before.

He dipped the cloth again. Out in the seawater something glinted. Something shifting in oily rainbow colours. Pools of black, whistling, wheezing. Wheezing as water rippled along and caught the air pockets on the edge of it.

Harry drew back. The new wave floated it in, a body, face down in the water. A stench of engine oil joined the corpse to the air. All its clothing was charcoaled, frayed by fire. Beyond it, drifting like huge clumps of seaweed thick with oil and petrol, were two more bodies, floating, riding in on the tide. They were brown, and slimy too… except for the faces. They had to be faces except the skin was brown and burned, and bright red where the mouth gaped in one last fatal gasp. Harry dropped the cotton strips and spiralled away in horror. But back up the beach behind him were those other heaps, and they were dead men too.

He turned away and suddenly, unexpectedly, up on the hill, glowing, white and bright and welcoming, was home. His own window, reflecting the rising sun, a beacon over the ruined village. He stared up with amazement and joy. Home. Still there. Still standing. And the box would be there. Right now no one would see him or stop him if he ran across the beach and into the village, and up the hill. He could rescue Daddy's photograph, go back to Totnes, and escape all this fighting and dying. Lewis could shout and rant, but Mum would see the photograph and remember, and that would change everything. But up on the dunes his GI friend lay injured and hidden.

Chapter Forty Seven

Splash! Moving the charred body in the shallows made Harry cringe. He searched its oily surface with trembling hands and brought a waterlogged back-pack to the surface. In it he found an army water canister, nearly full, and a food provisions tin, the ring pull kind. He cut away charred fabric with his penknife to release the water canister's safety chain.

The dead man's swollen eyes watched him with a glazed kind of calm. Harry drew back for a moment, uncertain and afraid. These troops were invaders. But what could this dead man do to him? Searching the body was strange, the deadness scary. Stiffness of muscles combined with limpness of flesh, body edges melting into the water, somehow fluid and dissolving. Part of the sea now, not the land. This was no person. No soldier. This was more a watery jellyfish kind of ghost. What if his dad…

He shook that horrible thought aside, but old Mr Thorn lying on his cottage floor crept in. Lonely, old and dusty, but somehow easier, more natural. He hadn't dared touch him. But now, right now, there was no choice. Mike needed water to drink and food to eat. He took a deep breath and pulled at the next pocket compartment, burned black. The fabric crumbled and bits stuck to his fingers. Inside was a sort of wallet thing. No time to examine it now. He shivered as he pocketed all his finds and waded out further.

This time he knew better what to expect and turned the body over deftly. He collected the water and food and went on to the third. By the time he was back by the landing craft and ready to crawl up to the hide, he was armed with treasure – a helmet full of fresh salt water, two tins of food and three canisters of drinking water. It would be enough for a day at least.

He only heard the jeep when its tyres crunched to a halt. He darted back out of sight but there was nowhere to hide. Footsteps approached on the shingle. He pressed back hard against the landing craft, angry he'd spent so much time down here, and gone so far out into the water.

'No despatches, Captain. No official reports. None! You hear me? And definitely no letters home about live ammunition.' The rasping voice had an American drawl.

'More bodies along here,' said an English

voice.

The two men stopped right by the end of the landing craft and looked back along the beach. He could see them clearly. A British officer, and an American one. A General maybe.

'Find who we want! Even one of those guys in the know is missing, the whole invasion's off.'

'Yes, sir.'

'And get the rest buried fast. I don't care where. Remember none of this ever happened.'

'Yes, sir.'

'Folks back home don't want to know their boys died on a British beach. Lock up any man who so much as whispers what he's seen.'

Harry pressed himself back harder against the hull, but the helmet still stuck out.

'Any man talks, I'll put a gun to his head.' The General struck the landing craft angrily with his fist. Clang!

One of the tins of bully beef fell from Harry's hand with a crunch onto the shingle. He squeezed his eyes shut and froze. But maybe the sound mingled in with the metal clang, or the crunch of the men's retreating footfalls. The jeep's engine started up, and it rattled away along the beach.

Chapter Forty Eight

The tourniquet was doing its job. The thigh wound had stopped bleeding, but blood was still seeping through from the shoulder. Harry wiped Mike's forehead and fed him water from a canister. He opened the blood soaked army shirt, slit away the vest beneath. 'Good salt seawater,' he explained as he washed the blood away. 'Daddy says it's antiseptic.' It looked like a bullet had gone right through the shoulder and out the other side. The hole was round with black edges and very deep. Scary.

He dabbed the wound again with the wet cloth. 'Remember Lewis the horrible Warden?' Mike's glazed eyes followed his every move. 'He chased me last night. I'm sure he was trying to get me exploded.' Mike winced. 'Does it hurt very bad?' He tried not to press so hard. 'He's sent my little sister away. Frightened Mum there would be bombs. We don't know where Peppy's gone. He won't tell us. Can that be right? Are you allowed to do that?'

He patted the bruised skin gently to dry it. 'Coming back last night, it's all... All the houses.

Everything's ruined. Why did they do that?' He laid a dry piece of cloth over the wound. 'Why are they loading dead bodies on trucks as if they're less important than cows?'

Mike moaned faintly, but he still didn't answer.

Harry thought of the two tins in his pocket. 'Look!' He held them up for Mike to see. 'What's Bully Beef?' He pulled the ring and the lid came off in one. The meaty smell hit the air, a more delicious aroma than he'd ever, ever smelt before, so strong it twisted his stomach and made his mouth water. He was ravenous, unstoppably hungry. He shovelled the meat greedily into his mouth with his fingers. Juice dribbled down his chin and he licked it back up with his tongue. Halfway down the tin he came to his senses. He leaned over Mike anxiously. 'Look, there's food.' He held it under Mike's nose but no reaction. He seemed to be asleep.

Up above, the sound of approaching engines. Harry sat back on his heels, frightened. He shook Mike's good shoulder, needing to know. 'Was last night the invasion? Why will that General shoot any man who talks?'

Chapter Forty Nine

A shaft of late afternoon sunlight burst through the clouds and lit up Start Bay as Celia came over the rise and glimpsed the familiar gold curve of Slapton Sands. But a strange haze of thick brown smoke hung over the Ley.

Suddenly she saw an army truck careering up the hill towards her. She crouched down behind gorse, praying they hadn't noticed her. The truck came to an abrupt stop nearby and the driver flung himself out. There was blood on his uniform. He was shaking. Another older GI leapt out after him. 'Let's take a walk, buddy,' he said. Celia ducked lower. They stopped right beside the gorse and stood looking down at the coastline. She held her breath.

'Our guys died on that beach.'

The friend lit up two cigarettes and passed one to the younger man. 'And if you mention it, the top brass will have your guts. Keep it together, pal.'

'We bury all our boys in mass graves so the enemy doesn't know we were here?'

'Your safety and mine, right? We follow

orders.'

'And they issue live ammunition for a rehearsal and don't tell us! Just let us kill each other so we can get the feel for battle? That ain't right. We got to tell someone what happened.'

'Don't be a fool.'

'So dig graves or face court martial. Swell choice!'

Behind the golden flowers Celia felt her scarf loosen. Like a tiny sail, it began picking up the breeze. She could feel the knot releasing and slipping, but if she dared to move... As if her thought transferred into a slight physical reaction, a twig suddenly cracked under her foot.

In a second they were on her, and the young one had her down with his gun pointing at her head. 'Don't shoot! Don't shoot!' she screamed, hearing a click of the safety catch coming off. 'I'm only looking for my son. Please don't shoot.'

The older GI stood over her. 'Who are you?'

Celia could feel the other one's gun trembling against her forehead. A jumpy, sweaty finger moved on the trigger. He was so close she could smell the blood on his uniform.

'Identity papers. My coat pocket.'

She felt him search nervously with his free hand and find it. He passed it up to the other.

'She heard us!' he said. The gun barrel still trembled against her skin.

'My son's missing,' she said, daring to speak. 'His name's Harry.'

There was silence as the older man examined the card. He stepped away. The gun stayed where it was.

'You're in a prohibited area, m'am.'

'My Harry's only a boy.'

The young GI stood up warily, but he was still aiming his revolver at her. He didn't take his finger off the trigger. 'There's a war on, lady.'

'And this is England,' she said.

'Right here is US territory.'

Keep calm, she told herself. Keep very calm. She stayed where she was on the ground, not daring to move. 'My Harry's down there,' she said. 'On Slapton Sands. He's been missing for two nights.'

'No one's been on that beach these last two nights, m'am.'

The young GI looked at his friend, tried hard to copy his steady approach. 'No,' he said nervously. 'No kids round there anymore. Not now.'

Celia dared to push herself up keeping her eyes on the gun. 'He'll be there. That's where he used to go all the time with his dad. We lived down there… or we did before…'

The young GI broke in. 'C'mon. We should shoot her.'

One wrong move and he might, she thought. He seemed frightened enough. 'Are you hurt?' she asked, looking at the blood on his uniform steadily and sympathetically.

The other one threw him a warning glance, and helped her up. 'Where've you come from?'

She risked brushing herself off, trying to gain their confidence by normal movements. 'I've walked from Totnes.'

'Well, m'am, you're just going to have to walk back.' He picked up her scarf and passed it to her. Their eyes met for an instant. She was very aware he thought she was pretty.

'We're supposed to shoot on sight,' said the other.

The older one ignored him. 'Your kid will be hiding somewhere back there,' he said to Celia.

'You think I haven't looked?' she cried.

'What'd you do to him?' asked the young GI, shifting about on his feet.

'Look, my husband's mis…' No, she thought quickly. Better '…he's fighting in Italy.'

'Sorry, m'am. Back to the road.'

266

'But Harry's on that beach, I know he is,' she protested, as they marched her back to the truck. There was sand and blood on its back platform, and a discarded, bloodied army boot.

'I don't think we should let her go,' said the jumpy one.

'Calm down,' hissed the other. 'We'll take her back to the limit.' He opened the truck door.

'No!' Celia insisted.

'I don't want to have to arrest you.'

'I've come so far!' she pleaded.

'I could shoot you.'

Tearfully she looked from one to the other. 'Don't you two have mothers?'

The younger GI glanced down at his gun, wiped his other hand down the bloodstain on his uniform.

'If it was your mother's young son lost in the middle of war? What would she do?' The older GI frowned and glanced inland across the hills.

It was the chance she needed, their momentary pang of conscience and homesickness. She sprinted back and leapt over the brow of the hill and away down the treacherous slope. A shot rang out across the landscape.

The GIs stared over the edge in horror brandishing their revolvers but there was nothing to aim at. The steep hill below was brilliant with yellow gorse. Celia was gone.

Chapter Fifty

There were shouts and a body was dragged past the bushes. Loose earth showered down into the hide. Harry crouched in the tiny floor space left to him, his hand clamped over Mike's mouth. Something strange was going on up there. With all the talk of shooting people, Mike was safer in here. Harry pulled his cramped legs in tighter and waited. The voices faded. All was quiet again.

'This is a good hide,' he whispered, as he checked Mike's thigh wound again. The bleeding had stopped a while back so he had loosened the tourniquet. Now the blood had congealed but the wound was still deep and dark under the cloth. Mike stirred.

'Are you okay?'

There was no real response, just a deep sigh.

The shoulder showed dark bruising now as well as the bullet hole, and the skin around it was burning hot to touch. Beads of sweat stood out on Mike's brow but he was shivering as if he was freezing cold. Harry tried to feed him the last drops from a water canister, but mostly it dribbled away out of the corner of his mouth. Very thirsty himself, he searched round for the other two canisters, forgetting they were both empty. He licked his dry lips, cross he hadn't rescued more water. 'When I was a little kid, my daddy and I used to play fighting games on this beach,' he said, trying to cheer up the situation with the sound of his own voice. 'You know, shooting each other.' He cocked his hand into a pretend gun. 'I never thought you could really die.' The words came out suddenly, seriously, without him thinking or choosing them. Then worse. 'If you don't hear anything, no letters, nothing, you know, from my dad. Does that mean someone's dead?' His hand trembled as he reached out to the helmet. The salt water in it was blood red now but at least it was cool. 'I think he is,' he said, dipping the cloth, squeezing the water out and laying it bloodstained across Mike's hot forehead 'I think he's shot like all those men last night. Like you.' Saying it out loud seemed to make it real. He leaned back against the cool rock, against the carved initials. A tear ran down his cheek. He smudged it away.

Outside he could hear the cries of seagulls close and then fading, then close again, circling.

'You shouldn't be on this beach.'

Harry jumped. Mike was staring across at him with glazed eyes. He had stopped shivering.

Harry leaned over him anxiously. 'You okay?'

Mike licked his lips and swallowed.

'There's no more water,' Harry said, wishing there was.

Mike took a deep wheezy breath. 'Where is everyone? Are they coming for me?'

Harry frowned. 'They're busy searching all the bodies, then dragging them away,' he said. 'Don't worry. You're safe.'

'No!' Mike's eyes were wide and angry. His hand shot out and held Harry's leg in a fierce grip. 'I need them to know. You got to go to them. But anything you've seen, anything they tell you, you forget. Right?'

Harry drew back, but Mike's fingers bit deeper into his flesh, hurting him. 'Forget?'

'Look, kid, you're caught up in secret stuff, but my outfit's got to know I'm here. Promise me!'

Harry nodded, trying to reassure him, trying to pull away.

'Promise!'

'Sure.'

Mike shook his arm urgently. 'Think of it like my mom needs to know I died on this beach.'

'Okay, okay.' The grip relaxed. The hand fell

away and Mike focussed on the rock. Harry waited. There was something weird about this conversation, the way Mike was talking, the rattle in his voice, how he looked. Frightening. 'But you're not dead,' he whispered.

'Should have written my number on my back like they did at Cold Harbour.'

Harry frowned. 'Where?'

Mike looked at him vacantly. 'Where am I?'

'This is my beach hide. I told you.'

'Yes.' Whatever demon had possessed Mike briefly was gone.

'There was an invasion last night,' Harry told him again. 'You know. Like William the Conqueror. Ten sixty-six. But who was it?'

Mike swallowed and closed his eyes. 'No ten sixty-six unit, kid,' he whispered. 'It was us. We came.'

'No, you were here on the beach.'

'In my pack.' Mike tried to shift but the effort was too much. 'You'll need my papers,' he breathed.

He'd forgotten about Mike's pack. It was more a shoulder bag than the duffle bags that were strapped to the bodies in the water. Against the hard cold surface of the rock it had served well as a pillow. Harry tried to pull it out, but it was caught under Mike's shoulder. Every tug made the GI writhe with pain. Harry sat back on his heels. If he couldn't free it, maybe he could cut into it. US army property and all that, but who was here to say he shouldn't? He pulled out his penknife and slit the side of the thick canvas open. Inside there was a proper army knife, some gum. Chocolate. And...

'Cola!' He pulled out the precious can triumphantly.

'Further in,' Mike whispered. 'Further.'

Harry leaned over him again. Right in under Mike's full weight he could feel something flat and dry. He tugged hard at it. Eventually he drew out a wallet. Mike's eyes followed it. 'Papers,' he confirmed, 'and...' Inside an American army identity card and a photograph.

Mike reached out for him again. 'Promise me, Harry Beere! Tell them I was here! We got to win this war. And they need those.'

'Okay. Okay.'

'Tell them, kid, but remember, you keep their secrets. Promise!'

The photo was Mike himself almost certainly, as a kid, with a woman. Longing suddenly washed over Harry for his own mum, her smile, the comfort of her arms round him. Photos did matter.

'Promise!' Mike demanded.

Harry passed him the photo. 'I promise.'

Mike sighed and shut his eyes. The hand clutching the photo fell back. His breathing quietened to almost nothing.

'Hey!' Harry shook him. He was cool suddenly and there was no reaction. 'Don't die,' he cried, 'don't die like my daddy.' He drew back staring at him. Mike lay very still.

After a long time Harry opened the cola and drank some. He ate the chocolate too. Angrily he wiped away an escaping tear, and then, so as not to think about what was happening, pushed the bush up to see out onto the beach, into the other weird world. The shore was clearer. The smoke had drifted inland. Now the last of the afternoon sunlight shone across the radius of the bay and twinkled in the shallows. It glinted on the beached landing craft and flashed off bits of twisted metal. On the dunes there were new scratch marks in the sand where dead men had been pulled away. Down on the shingle officers were turning more bodies over quickly, roughly, as if to spend too much time over them was dangerous. After they were searched, they were dragged away. Other uniformed men wearing round white helmets were inspecting bodies all the way along the beach.

Harry could hear snippets of conversation. 'Before we're even fighting...' The voices had a familiar drawl. 'they say we've lost at least seven hundred... eight.' 'Shut-up... it was nothing but a storm, remember?' Down by the landing craft two GIs pulled the three bodies out of the water. A cloud passed over the sun as they laid them out on the shingle and an officer came and searched them. Two were borne off on stretchers towards the trucks. The next was inspected a second time, and a third, before his body was finally hauled away.

The evening tide was bringing in more.

Marines splashed into the shallows to pull in a lifeboat. Men from it covered in blood and oil collapsed onto the shingle, dazed, heads in hands. Others were carried up the beach, but any man who could walk was immediately ordered to take dead bodies to nearby army trucks. There were US officers directing activity, organising, but the men worked slowly and did not obey easily. One man from the lifeboat staggered up the beach towards the hide. His uniform was just like Mike's. Harry ducked down. Just short of the bushes the marine sank gratefully into the soft sand of the dune, close enough for Harry to hear his breathing. Dripping oil and seawater, and smelling of fire, for a long time he just sat there, silently surveying the scene. 'For God's sake we were only practising,' he said quietly.

He began to sing softly. 'Oh, say can you see, by the dawn's early light, What so proudly we hailed at the twilight's last gleaming? Whose broad stripes and bright stars, through the perilous fight...

Harry had heard the US anthem before. Through the bushes he watched the marine put his hand on his heart. 'O say, does that star-spangled banner yet wave O'er the land of the free and the home of the brave?'

Harry slid back down to Mike and shook him. 'You can't die!' he whispered. 'The guys who came onto the beach. It wasn't a real invasion, was it? That's what you meant. They were Americans like you, weren't they?' But Mike lay still.

Chapter Fifty One

The two GIs thundered along in the truck, scanning the landscape against the red sunset. Their quarry would have to break cover somewhere at the bottom of the hill.

'There she is!'

They swerved into flat land, jumped out and gave chase. Unable to outrun them, Celia was soon caught.

'Let me go back to my house,' she pleaded, struggling to get free. 'Harry will go there. I know he will. Let me look!'

As they marched her back towards their truck, a US jeep pulled up. An officer leapt out. 'What's going on?' he demanded.

The GIs let go of her, guilt written all over their faces.

'Who is this woman?'

She faced her captors with utter joy. 'No way out now,' she said triumphantly. 'Someone else knows I'm here. You're going to have to take me into Slapton!'

Chapter Fifty Two

Harry slept fitfully, his head lolling on Mike's chest. He dreamed of running on the sand in burning sunlight. Of golden windows and screaming gulls over oil black water. The wind breathed. The beach heaved itself into new and confusing shapes he couldn't recognise. He dreamed of war games and mock battles and arrows flying. And an eye, as wide as the bay, as red as blood. Of a puppet dancing on the shingle and a penknife slicing its strings. It folded down. Lay still. When he turned it over it had Daddy's face. He woke up wet with sweat and grief. A new day beamed in through the crevices. Under him Mike lay still and cool.

For a long time Harry sat back against the rock, his knees up tight, staring at Mike's body. If he hadn't shouted out his name, the GI might not have turned, might not have been shot. Dragging him here, hiding him, none of his efforts had been enough. Wounds must be clean. What if he'd added germs from his vest? Maybe with bodies and petrol in it, the seawater wasn't antiseptic like it should be. 'Private Mike White! United

278

States Marines. Nice to be acquainted, Harry Beere.' If he'd left him out on the beach, his smiling GI friend might still be alive.

But if those men storming the beach were US troops, and it was GIs like Mike on the dunes, why were they killing each other? And why shoot anyone who talked about it now?

Well, he was going to have to talk about it. He'd made a solemn promise. Otherwise this hide would be a grave. Mike would be listed missing, and his mom would never know what had happened. He swallowed hard and remembered Mike saying afraid was somewhere for brave to begin. They might shoot him, but he had to tell.

He smeared away his tears and looked out over the dunes again. The singing GI was long gone, and all the bodies had been cleared. The trucks were miles away down the beach. He drained the can of cola, pocketed Mike's papers and the rest of the chocolate, and without wanting to look back, reached up and pushed the bush aside. The sun was up, streaking the sky with gold. The Ley reflected it back like a mirror.

To reach the troops at the other end of the beach was a long walk. Slapton wasn't far. But Torcross was closest, and it was home. Go there.

GIs would be there surely. If he used the dipped path behind the dunes to the village, and spotted Lewis, he could hide. He climbed out and scrambled down into the scrub.

Chapter Fifty Three

Guarded like a criminal in a small isolated basement room, Celia waited all night, thinking.

No letters, no news, for months now. Her John was gone. She cried for him, ached for him, but there was still no word. Nothing to keep her hopes alive. He was dead like the rest.

There was no family now. And since they'd left here, not even friends. Amy, dear Amy, somewhere out of Exeter. Poor Miss Markham, dead. Faith Gale, would she really put up with her sister? And where was Kathleen, with that huge sideboard?

She knew she was wasting her time with those high brow voluntary service women in Totnes. She was just a country girl. Going out, going anywhere, enjoying anything in war time, none of that was the done thing for them. And any men who smiled at her would suddenly look away afraid. She could swear they were imagining how quickly other men would smile at their own wives while they were away fighting.

There was Lewis. Calling her weak and silly and afraid, unable to think for herself, and always insisting he knew what was best for her, but providing for her. On the one hand intense and possessive, and very protective. On the other, a difficult, vindictive man. She might learn to cope with his temper, but could she expect her children to? And sending Peppy away?

Now at midday she was called.

'Harry is here, I know it!'

'I can assure you, m'am, there is no child here in Slapton, nor at Torcross.'

She persevered, frantic to make them understand. 'But I'm certain he's here. It's his home.' She faced them, holding her nerve against these four officers, all lined up in their smart US uniforms and stout army boots, with the authority to hold her against her will.

'You escaped the custody of the US Army.'

'I wasn't aware I was in custody. This is not a police state.'

'There's a war on,' said the one English officer with them.

'I'm looking for my son.'

'You entered into a prohibited area, ma'am. Requisitioned land, as I'm sure you're aware.'

'What's going on here?' cried Celia. 'Why won't you help me?'

'You should have informed the proper

authorities in Totnes.'

'I did. They took no notice.'

They were going round and round. 'There's a terrible lot of damage,' she said suddenly. 'Is that why you're all so secretive?' Wrong question. Any sympathy they had evaporated. She glanced out of the window, wishing she hadn't pointed out the obvious, frightened how they might react now. British soldiers were passing the gate. With them was a face she knew.

'Lewis,' she cried joyfully. 'He'll tell you! He knows me!'

'Who?'

'The Warden.' She pointed out the window. Lewis was fetched immediately. He glowered at her, furious to be drawn in.

'Mrs Beere appealed to me back in December to help her find accommodation in Totnes,' he said, shifting nervously from one foot to the other. 'As Area Warden I made enquiries and was able find suitable rooms for her and her children.'

'He helped us move,' said Celia, urgently demonstrating his involvement. Couldn't he see she needed help? 'He drove us. And he paid the rent sometimes.'

The senior officer raised an eyebrow. 'And was that in an army car, Warden?'

'Yes,' said Celia. Lewis went bright red and shot her an angry glance. 'We were all forced out of our homes with nowhere to go,' she said accusingly, 'so you Americans could move in.'

The eyes dipped and focused on Lewis again. 'Was there further contact?'

'The landlady complained to me that the boy was always snooping about.'

'Snooping about?' cried Celia indignantly.

'He was seen talking to a prisoner of war at one of the farms.'

'A boy, his own age! He told me!'

'I paid the landlady a bit of rent to pacify her. I thought nothing of it at the time. There was no reason for me to get involved. It was just an accommodation.'

Celia stared at him.

'Warden, do you know of any reason why the boy might have returned to this area now?'

'No, sir.'

'You do know! The photo of his father,' Celia reminded him. 'We left it behind.'

The senior officer narrowed his eyes at Lewis.

'What photo?' Lewis asked, looking mystified.

'You remember!' cried Celia.

'The boy was a violent little tearaway as I remember. Dangerous kid.'

'Lewis!'

'During the past two days, Warden, have you seen this boy?'

'No, sir,' said Lewis.

'It was the one photo we had of my husband,' she pleaded. 'He's missing in Italy. Harry idolised him.'

The senior officer sighed. 'Mindful of the …er…situation, have you seen anyone other than military personnel today, Warden?'

Lewis glanced curtly at Celia and back to the senior officer. 'No, sir.'

'You've seen me!' cried Celia.

'Anyone, Warden?'

'No one, sir,' said Lewis.

'Dismiss.'

Lewis left the room. Celia stared after him in utter disbelief. The British officer followed him out. The others, the Americans, turned back to her.

'What other reason would you have for returning to this area, m'am?'

'Let me go back to my house,' she pleaded, very afraid now. 'Please! Harry will go there. I know he will.'

Outside the window was a sudden commotion as a young GI staggered into the drive. The

British officer with Lewis, just emerging from the building, rushed to help.

'That's White!' said the senior officer urgently.

Before she was ushered quickly away, Celia saw the marine's uniform was bloodied and torn. He faltered as Lewis reached him as if he recognised him. Unexpectedly, with every last ounce of strength he hit out at him. 'That's for the kid.' Lewis fell back stunned clutching his jaw as the GI collapsed into the British Officer's arms.

Chapter Fifty Four

In the empty shell that had been the post office the rubble crunched under Harry's feet. Every fallen beam and shifting brick seemed to whisper, 'There is a war on, you know.' He climbed the last obstacle to reach the jagged edges of the split lathe-and-plaster wall overlooking the road. Part of a brick wall fell behind him. Except to silence his thoughts of Miss Markham, the crash brought no response. No GI. There was no sign of anyone. Maybe the thud and dust of falling buildings was commonplace, going unnoticed now.

Along the coast road a lone covered jeep approached. Harry ducked behind rubble and waited. He heard it stop, and muffled sounds of conversation. Maybe someone got out. Eventually when he chanced a look, the jeep had started off again. There was no sign of anyone staying behind. The jeep drove on round behind the Ley. He thought of flagging it down on its return, but what if it was Lewis? He hid as it passed. It drove away along the coast road again, heading for the far end of the beach. Distance made the troops there look like ants milling round a nest. He'd just missed his best chance to reach them.

He stared around his ruined village. The thatched cottage that had survived the original bomb was flattened. So was the old Jubilee hall where week by week he'd gazed hopefully at newsreels. The tearoom that once served sweet fruit jam and clotted cream scones was gone. And the corner shop where Mrs Prouse made her living, where Frank had his power base. All the seafront buildings were destroyed. Americans were dead on the beach. What was left here to come back to?

There was one thing. He sprinted over the craters and rubble and up round the corner. There it was, the cottage his father built, its white-washed front wall glowing in the midday sun. He was home. The prize he had come for was moments away! He could rescue it, make sure Mike was found, then take the photo back. Daddy would make everything all right. Mum would look at his face and remember.

There was damage, window glass broken, shaken out of the frames by so much shelling. He darted past his own window, swishing his hand against the dusty blackout curtain that hung listlessly through it. Breathless and excited, he turned the handle and flung open the front door.

Everything behind was fallen away. Only the front gable wall where he stood remained. Clinging tightly together with a few last nails, it cloaked the real truth, tricking him into believing the whole cottage still existed. There were no rear walls. No roof. Just clear blue sky. His room was gone, the kitchen, his mother's room upstairs. All just piles of timbers and stones and debris. And underneath somewhere was his box. He climbed into the rubble, remembering the box had been waiting near the front door. Desperately he tossed the wood and stones aside there, but turned up only bricks, and stones, then a chair leg, crushed and splintered. He tore faster through the debris, choking on the rising dust. A twisted lump of metal emerged, once the kitchen towel hook. Further down sharp slivers of his mother's bedroom mirror flashed a warning as they caught the reflection of the sky. Nothing was where it might have been. Falling in, the cottage had rearranged its contents. Somewhere under it all, hopelessly beyond finding, were the fragile treasures in his box. The shells and the driftwood would be crunched and splintered and shattered. And all of them would combine to break the glass and slice through the paper image of his father. He stopped digging. Somehow the remembered photo began to shrink and go pale, like a ghost blowing away into the distance. Everything he believed in was fading. There was nothing left to hold on to. He dropped down onto the rubble in despair.

Suddenly he snatched back his breath and listened. Yes, there it was again. A footstep. He turned. Framed by the doorway, silhouetted and black against the bright midday light, was a shape he recognised instantly.

Chapter Fifty Five

'Where are we going?' he cried, as Lewis bundled him along the road.

'Don't try anything. We're shooting intruders on sight.'

'Everyone?' They were heading down towards the deserted beach.

'Everyone.'

'Kids?'

Lewis's grip on him hurt. But there was no one else. Harry took a deep breath and kept his promise. 'There's a GI out in the dunes. He...' He thought quickly. Maybe they wouldn't go back for just dead people. 'He's badly hurt. He needs help. I'll show you where he is.'

'Don't give me all that rubbish. Come on.'

'It's not rubbish,' Harry cried, frantically struggling to get free. 'Help him, please! I pulled him off the beach.'

Lewis ignored his pleas and marched him on.

'Mike's sick! Please listen to me!'

'You young tearaway!' Lewis tightened his grasp so Harry could hardly breathe. 'It's high time you knew what punishment was, boy.'

Harry struck out, catching Lewis on the stomach. 'You can shoot me if you want to, but I'm telling you there's a GI on the beach.'

Lewis hauled him in close. There was a dark bruise on his jaw. 'Look,' he said, his breath hot on Harry's face, 'You're not telling anyone anything. I'm making sure of that. Who'd believe you anyway?'

There was a sudden blast. Lewis looked up. Harry wrenched away from his grip and ran.

Lewis gave chase, but Harry was too fast, running like lightning towards the Ley. When he knew Lewis couldn't see him, he darted up the slope and into the old bomb shelter.

Everything was ominously quiet.

'Kid?' Lewis was stamping around somewhere down by the cottages. Breathless, Harry pulled the old shelter door shut. It dropped in its rusty hinges with a sigh.

'Go to hell then, wherever you are.' Lewis's shouting echoed through the ruined cottages. 'You're on your own. Celia can search all she likes now. Secrecy rules here.'

'What?' Harry pushed at the door. It didn't move. He flung his weight at it, but it was jammed shut. 'What?' he yelled. 'Lewis?'

All he could think of was his mum's pretty

face, her hand ruffling his hair, smell the gentle sweetness of her. Daddy's picture wouldn't be enough. He couldn't give it to her anyway, but he could hug her, say sorry for all the horrible things he'd said to her, rescue her from Lewis, stick with her. Together they could rescue Peppy. If his mum was somewhere out there searching for him, he had to find her fast.

'Lewis?'

Chapter Fifty Six

There were pinpricks of light round the bolts but Harry could feel the door itself was swollen and damaged. No amount of pushing would budge it.

Further back, the damp earth packed close round the walls smelled like happy days of digging. The shed was set snugly into the slope. If he could pull away any of the corrugated iron wall, earth would fall straight in on him. In whatever direction he would have to dig himself out. And there was no time.

No light showed in the curved roof above him. That was two strong layers of curved metal, and there was earth above that too. He and Dad helped old Mr Thorn put it there. This wasn't an Anderson shelter, but it was as safe as it could be, and no one wanted to believe tiny Torcross was a target even when the bombers flew directly overhead. The old battery gun at the far end of the beach often fired optimistically into the dark nights, but it was Plymouth and Dartmouth, the naval docks and the battle ships the enemy wanted.

He felt for the old light switch on the

supporting post. But the electric had been turned off with the evacuation, and with all the devastation, what chance of power now? He stamped in fury on the old wooden floor. A thin line of daylight appeared. He stared down at it in surprise. He stamped again. A crunch. The line was wider. He crouched down. The wood here was damp and rotten. He pulled at it. It crumbled in his fingers. He grasped a chunk. It splintered and broke away. He tore up more. And then more. Daylight. A void between the floor and the earth. He lay down and put his head into the hole.

He could see, and now he remembered it too, a step down outside to ground level made of a row of loose stones. Light filtered through the space between them. There were joists on those, and then this wooden floor, suspended on them. The shed was meant to be strong but it wasn't. If he could get rid of more of the floor, and it could be weak enough here, he might be able to slide under, push out two or three of those stones. He'd have to be careful because the corner could collapse on him but there might just be enough room to squeeze out.

But there was something sticking in through a gap at the end. He caught his breath recognising three red sticks of dynamite, bound together. Through another gap he saw a long wire cable stretching away across the sloping earth outside.

He grabbed his penknife out of his pocket and punched urgently into the rotten floor.

Chapter Fifty Seven

'You weren't notified your husband was dead?'

Celia, her face streaked with tears, shook her head. 'How? We weren't here, were we?'

The US officer frowned and glanced across at his CO sitting behind the cluttered desk.

'Where is my son?' she pleaded.

The CO thumped the desk angrily. 'He pulled a serving soldier off the battlefield!' His voice had a strong Southern drawl.

'We were all through, sir,' the US officer argued. 'And we had moved right along the beach.'

'The kid had no right to be there, Kennedy,' snapped the other. 'You know as well as I do what's at stake.'

'He bathed Mike White's injuries.'

'And damn near killed him.'

'That's not what White says. If he'd been left on that beach he'd have bled to death long before we came back for him.'

'Stop it,' Celia cried. 'If some Italian child had pulled my John off the battlefield he might still be alive!'

The CO rounded on her. 'Be realistic. It's not a game for kids. This is war, Mrs Beere.'

'Realistic? Lewis Cramer arranged for my daughter's evacuation somewhere I don't know. My son is out on your so called battlefield and you don't know where he is! And everything you've broken and destroyed here is my home.'

'Home? This is not your home, lady. This is requisitioned US military territory.'

'You're not British! It's not yours!'

'A lot of our guys died out there last night for the sake of the British.'

'Shut up, Kennedy!' The CO glared at him.

In the distance there was an explosion.

Celia screamed and covered her face with her hands. 'When will it ever stop?' she cried. 'My mother was bombed. John's family too. How many generations of us will it take? My father died in the trenches in the last war, and his father too. You tell me today my husband's not just missing but dead in this one. I want my son.'

The CO looked at her. 'I'm afraid...'

'You don't know what it is to be afraid. Nobody thinks about the women left behind. No money, no home, no love. You men all go off to your wars and leave us. And die!'

Both men stared at her helplessly. She hit the

desk with a clenched fist. 'If you're fighting for any kind of future, help me find my Harry!'

The CO pushed his chair away from the desk and stood glaring out the window. Here he was, under orders from the General to preside over a nightmare, a catalogue of errors. Failed communications between ships, uncoordinated timings, unexpected enemy attack at sea. Operation Tiger, a real life rehearsal for the D-Day landings to make inexperienced men ready for battle, but with men on the beach unaware they were using live ammunition to repel a mock invasion. It all beggared belief, a complete and total disaster! Now he was expected to find the last of the dozen men privy to Allied planning, dead or alive, and secretly bury nearly a thousand soldiers and marines in mass unmarked graves. And for the sake of the coming invasion of Europe, and Allied morale, bury the truth along with them.

There was another muffled explosion. Celia caught her breath again, terrified. Kennedy glanced uneasily at his CO 'They're blowing up unexploded shells down there.'

'Look,' said the CO. 'I'll get you out of here, that's the best I can do.'

She shook her head. 'It's not enough. I won't

go without Harry.'

He looked angrily at his watch and then at Kennedy. 'We have to locate the kid. She's your responsibility. Keep her out of sight where possible. Any man so much as mentions her, he's in the brig. No second chances. Shoot her if she runs. And I mean that, Kennedy. You have one hour.'

Chapter Fifty Eight

Half way along to Torcross a truck blocked the coast road.

'Keep down,' Kennedy warned. In the back of the covered jeep, Celia pulled the tarpaulin over her head again and crouched low and flat behind his seat.

'Going through, soldier,' she heard him say.

'Sorry, blowing up live shells, sir. No go.'

'Wish I had a choice,' said Kennedy. 'CO's orders.'

There was a moment's deliberation while the GI consulted. The engine was rattling underneath her, and the temperature was rising in her dark confined hiding place. She breathed carefully and very slowly, trying to keep as still as possible.

'Okay, but watch out!' A shout. 'Back up, boys. He's going through.' She heard an engine growl as the truck was pulled out of the way. 'The disposal guys are along at the end of the lake.'

'Ley,' said Kennedy. 'They call it a Ley.'

'Ley. Lake. That's where they are.'

The jeep bounced forward again. 'Right,' said Kennedy after a minute, 'better come out and think where to look.' She emerged to see him pat the passenger seat. 'I know the couple of guys working along here. They'll keep their mouths shut.'

She climbed across, pleased to be breathing cool sea air again, and looked ahead. But Torcross wasn't there! The end of the bay where it should be was, and the hill leading up from that. But the village was ruined, almost entirely gone. It shocked her, the devastation. There wasn't anywhere left for Harry to hide.

'What have you done?' she said tearfully.

'Where to?' asked Kennedy, as if he hadn't heard.

'He'd go home,' she said, her voice breaking with emotion. 'Our cottage is up the hill, a turning off near the shops.' But there were no shops. No post office. No houses along the beach. There was a corner where the dusty road turned up past a high heap of rubble. Kennedy veered round it.

'Look! Look!' Celia cried, as she saw the white façade of the cottage. 'Let me out!' She was out of the jeep and running as soon as Kennedy stopped. 'Harry!' she shouted.

'Hey!' Kennedy leapt out after her, pulling out his revolver. By the time he reached her, she was standing at the open door, shocked at the scene behind. 'They said we could come back!' she cried. 'They said they only wanted our village for training.' She fell to her knees, clawing at the rubble.

For a moment Kennedy let her dig, then he crouched down beside her. 'White said he was on the beach, remember?' She looked up at him through her tears. 'Give up on this one,' he said. 'Your boy's not here.' He helped her up. 'I don't know why the CO let you do this,' he said. 'Guess he hasn't heard from his own wife in a while.'

She clambered back to the door. 'Old Mr Thorn's,' she said. 'He went there gardening every day after school.'

The cottages along by the Ley had been pretty. It was heartbreaking to see them in ruins. Behind them, the terraced gardens her John had helped to build were now desolate craters. Smoke hung on the air. Nearby two disposal guys were packing up, loading equipment back onto their truck. Kennedy asked one of them if they'd seen a kid.

'Hell, no. We've been dynamiting. There were a lot of unexploded shells round here,' he said. 'Who's she?'

'Open your mouth about her to anyone, you're dead, soldier,' said Kennedy. 'Either one of you.'

The guy smirked. 'Yeah. Sure.'

Kennedy reached for his revolver. 'CO's orders.'

'Okay, okay, keep your shirt on.' He threw some detonators to his mate in the truck. 'Okay by you, Will?'

Will nodded. 'I see nothing, Harvey.'

Celia scanned what was left of the road round the Ley, her heart sinking. 'There was a shelter,' she said, remembering suddenly and looking up the slope. 'He'd go there. He'd know that would be safe.'

Harvey shook his head. 'Gone,' he said. 'Unexploded stuff up there. We couldn't take the chance. We blew it all.'

But she was already scrambling up. 'It was a bomb shelter. It's possible.'

The metal front and door were torn and twisted. The explosion had ripped right through the rest and the splintered timbers still smouldered. The corrugated iron roof was in shreds, collapsed inwards taking all the earth down with it. A blast in such a confined space – anyone inside would be blown to pieces.

'You British sure are optimists,' said Kennedy,

examining a jagged piece of wood.

Celia staggered down the slope in tears. 'I don't know where else to look,' she said. 'There's nothing left here.'

Kennedy looked at his watch. 'We've only got a few more minutes,' he said.

'Down there,' she said suddenly, wiping her tears with the back of her hand. She pointed along to the sea front rubble. He followed her doubtfully as she strode towards the collapsed post office. 'We can get through here to the beach,' she said.

Kennedy shook his head firmly. 'No m'am. That's way off limits.'

'Hey!' Will was running after them. 'Harvey found these,' he said. 'US identity. We're supposed to hand them in. Might as well send them back with you, sir.' He held out two sets of papers.

Kennedy opened them. One was singed and quite waterlogged. The other had blood on it. 'Where did he find this one?'

'Up by that shelter after we'd blown it.'

'What?' she asked, looking at Kennedy's face and suddenly going cold. 'What?'

'It's White's, the guy the kid was with.'

'Harvey found this up there too,' said Will,

holding out a grimy penknife.

'It's Harry's!'

They both looked at her. She was shaking. Kennedy took the penknife and pressed it into her hand. She felt it ice cold in her palm. It was almost too heavy to hold, as if she was weighed down by it, and it might make her sink down under the earth.

Kennedy caught her arm to support her.

'He's dead,' she whispered. 'My Harry is dead.'

Chapter Fifty Nine

'Come on,' Kennedy said, leading her gently back towards the jeep. 'I'll pass these papers to the CO,' he called back to Will.

She struggled, pleading with him. 'The beach, the beach. Let me go down there.'

He shook his head.

'Please,' she begged. 'Harry loved it so much. It was his. I need a few moments. He walked on that beach every day, just like his father. I need to see it one more time.' She looked up him, willing him to let her. 'I'll go after that, I promise. Anywhere you send me. I don't want to come back here ever.'

Kennedy glanced back. The two disposal guys were both by the truck now, busy finishing up.

'Let me, please,' she begged. 'Please.'

He consulted his watch. 'You'll have me slaughtered,' he said. 'Go on, then.'

Kennedy was close behind as she climbed over the rubble of the post office, and down onto the shingle, feeling it crunch down under her shoes. Everywhere there were craters filled with deep dark sand, and drips and smears of blood across the white pebbles. Something terrible had happened here. She glanced round fearfully. Two landing craft, like stranded whales, lay abandoned in the shallows. Only when she was past them and right down by the water's edge did the beach seem safe and clean. She began to stride along. Kennedy gave her space, kept back.

The sea washed in and out, jostling the pebbles. Sometimes it broke through in a swirl before it dragged away leaving the shingle glistening wet and washed. Soon it would fill in the craters and cover the awful secrets, whatever they were. She stared along the deserted shore. How many times had she seen Harry running along this beach? He had taken his first steps here, and as a little boy, danced in and out of the waves every summer. All his life he'd been a beach child, collecting shells and old bits of driftwood, attached to this shore like some sea creature. Even in the worst winter weather he loved to walk along the sand dunes, just like his father. Her John was gone, and now Harry was too. She stopped in her tracks, filled with such a sense of loss she could no longer contain it. She lifted her head and howled up into the sky. 'Harry! Harreee!'

There was nothing but silence and the sea. The

water washed up near her feet and pulled back down across the shingle. It washed in closer and dragged back again, rattling over the pebbles, as if the sea was drawing breath.

'Mum!'

Now she knew she was going mad. She could even hear him calling her. She knew she would hear him calling her forever.

'Mum!'

Wanting him, was she conjuring him up? She swung round. On the dunes he was, climbing up and out of the sand somehow. She started to run.

'Hey,' shouted Kennedy. 'Stop! I have my orders.'

She ran faster not caring about his orders or guns or war.

Kennedy chased her, snatching out his revolver. It was something he'd never thought he'd ever do, shoot a woman, and he hated the CO for it. He'd said she would run and he was damn right. He made his choice and took aim. But along his line of sight there was something else.

'Mum!' Harry ran with the speed of wind, as if the tide and sky were carrying him forward. She was all he could see, all he wanted to see. 'Mum!' he shouted. 'Mum!' 'Harry!' She was running towards him, crying out his name. He leapt into her outstretched arms, swung round and round, then they were hugging, and pulling back laughing all out of breath, and then holding each other close again.

Kennedy skimmed pebbles out into the water, bounce, bounce, bounce, across the surface. Now he turned and marched towards them, his smart US army boots crunching down into the pale accepting shingle. 'Back to headquarters,' he said.

'Will they kill me, Mum?' whispered Harry, as they followed Kennedy up the beach.

'No!' She hugged him again.

'Lewis chased me and said they'll shoot me.'

'Lewis?' She glared back towards the village, filled with fury. 'I never want to see that horrible Lewis again.'

'I'm sorry I ran away. I wanted the photo of Daddy for you. For Peppy. But it's all rubble at home. Everything's fallen in.'

'I know,' she said. 'We've only got our memories now.' Her face was so serious, so beautiful. 'Your dad's dead, Harry. For certain. They told me today.'

'I sort of knew ages ago,' he said, needing to breathe very deeply.

'I sort of knew too,' she said. 'And I've been so afraid.'

'It's all my fault.'

'It's not your fault! Daddy went because he thought it was the right thing to do.' She knelt down, holding him tight. 'Oh Harry, it frightens me what awful things you've seen on this beach. You've been so brave.'

He leaned in against her, suddenly overcome by tears. 'There's a GI, Mum. Mike.' He searched his pockets in vain for Mike's papers. 'His mum has to know he died here on the beach. I've promised.'

'Is that the GI you saved?'

'But I didn't save him. He's dead like Daddy. He's gone from the hide, but I know he's dead.'

'No, Harry! He's in Slapton. He's alive.'

Chapter Sixty

'Look, soldier, the kid's seen too much,' the CO said gravely. 'If Eisenhower knew…'

White nodded. 'Eisenhower's not here now.'

'The outcome of this war hinges on complete secrecy. My orders…'

'He's a kid, sir!'

'Right now,' said the CO angrily, 'is no time for sentiment. I can't risk thousands of men's lives.'

A knock and the door opened. 'Kennedy's back.'

As soon as Harry saw Mike, he rushed to him. 'I thought you were dead. My daddy's dead. I thought you were too.'

Mike held him as close as he could. 'It's okay. It's okay. See? I'm bandaged up!'

'I went to tell them like I promised, so your mum would know, but the only person I could find was Lewis and he wouldn't listen. He said they'd shoot me.'

Mike glanced across at Celia. 'He's a good kid.'

'Harry,' she said, 'we can't ever talk to anyone about what we've seen. What you've seen. Ever. Not even about your GI friend here. It's secret.

I've promised. They say lots of men's lives are depending on us, maybe the whole war. We can keep their secret, can't we?'

'Yes,' he said. 'I promised Mike.'

'For ever? It might be forever. Even from Peppy.'

'Mike is my friend. I promised him.'

She turned back to them all. 'My son is brave, you've seen that. He'll keep your secrets as long as you want.'

The CO looked her straight in the eye. 'But can you?'

'I have no choice,' she said, 'Harry's my son.'

'I've got to look after my mum, now,' said Harry.

Mike nodded. 'Your dad would be real proud of you, Harry Beere.'

'Sir, you said you'd get them out of here,' said Kennedy.

The CO stood staring out the window. The spire of Slapton Church pointed into the clear blue English sky. Up near the army camp, lush green hills glistened in the afternoon sun. 'We Americans want peace too, Mrs Beere. Then we can all go home to our wives and kids.'

Harry and Celia waited hand in hand. 'I have no

idea where we're going now,' she said, 'but we'll find our darling Peppy, and start again. And never speak about this, to any one.'

'We will remember Daddy though, won't we, Mum?'

There were tears in her eyes. 'Oh Harry, not a day will go past.'

Harry smelled the fresh salty tide coming in. It might wash away all the blood and the fighting, but somehow the beach wasn't his now. It belonged to all those men who had died on it. 'One day we'll come back though and I'll build a new cottage. Daddy said we belong here.'

She squeezed his hand. 'One day, maybe.'

'And Mike. I can't forget him.'

'He'll never forget you. He told me.'

'Mike says that's the best,' Harry said, 'when the people who love you remember you.'

The secret of the beach was kept for nearly fifty years.

Some thirty thousand men of the US Army and the US Navy with little experience of fighting or war took part in the ill-fated rehearsals for D Day on Slapton Sands in Devon in April 1944. Nearly a thousand lost their lives. The tragedy was covered up. Painful lessons were learned. A few weeks later during the actual D-Day assault landings on Utah beach, only some two hundred men were killed.

6th June 1944: D-Day marks start of Europe invasion.

This is the news, read by John Snagge. D Day has come! Early this morning the Allies began the assault on the north western face of Hitler's European fortress. The first official news came just after half past nine when Supreme Headquarters of the Allied Expeditionary forces landed on the Normandy beaches…

Sources and References

The Gate of The Year
by Minnie Louise Haskin from her Volume The
Desert 1908

King George VI
Extracts from Christmas Broadcast 1943

Winston Churchill:
Extract from World broadcast 31 August 1943
Extract from World broadcast March 26th 1944

wight diamond press

www.wightdiamondpress.com

Cutting In
Felicity Fair Thompson

Ambition can take over your life. Ballet is no ordinary career for Elaine, more a magnificent obsession. Insecure and unloved, she is desperate to prove herself. Watching the beautiful Beverley dance, she imitates, borrows, steals, wanting everything Beverley has. Each movement. Every reaction. Each smile. To stalk in pursuit of an image. There's no threat in that, surely? Eighteen, it's a dangerous age, when a girl has to cut her way into life.

One of the three top finalists in the Beryl Bainbridge Award, People's Book Prize 2012/13

'Hard edged, striking and truthful.'
Best selling novelist Julian Rathbone
'Poignant and believable.'
Averil Ashfield, Transworld Books
'A great gift for portraying the agonies and ecstasies of adolescence. A rare talent.'
Frederick E Smith, Best Selling Novelist and Screen Writer
'I read it at a single sitting. Perceptive writing wonderfully spiked with bitchiness.'
Graham Hurley, Crime Writer

0-9535123-0-4

Hold Tight
Felicity Fair Thompson

A wall of window high up. The child watches the night close in, several times huffing against the glass to mist it up, pressing her hand into the condensation and watching the imprint slowly fade.

When a small child is abducted, WPC Jane Velalley shares the long cruel hours of waiting with the distraught mother. With her own home life in turmoil, and facing escalating criminal activity and emotional distress, Velalley must use all her energy and wits, and still hold tight to everything she loves and values most herself.

'Unputdownable! A novel and screenplay rolled into one. It had me on the edge of my seat. Fantastic!'
Michelle Magorian Author of 'Goodnight Mister Tom'
'Gripping and emotional read, I couldn't put it down.'
Writer Mary Grand
'Beautifully crafted. Really perceptive descriptions.'
D.M. Australia
'A well crafted, emotional novel.'
Writer Lucy Blanchard

978-0-9535123-3-1

The Inspiration for
The Kid on Slapton Beach

Felicity Fair Thompson

Children all over the world are caught up in wars. So many people have to leave their homes and everything they know behind.

The tank by the Ley at Torcross in Devon is real and in World War 2 Exercise Tiger is historic fact. I wanted to explore what could happen to a young fictional character set against the tragedy of the D-Day rehearsals on Britain's Slapton Sands.

'Superb on so many levels... a wonderful book.'
Michelle Magorian Author of 'Goodnight Mister Tom'
'A great read that rushes to a brilliant climax!'
John Ovenden ABC Broadcaster and Journalist Australia
'...a pivotal moment in the war...'
Joint Forces Journal USA
'A great story and very well told.'
Anna Home Chair of the Children's Film and Television Foundation
'This book is beautiful. A jewel!'
Actress June Brown, Dot in East Enders.

978-0-9535123-2-4